ROMAN LEGIONS ON THE MARCH

SOLDIERING IN THE ANCIENT ROMAN ARMY

HADRIAN'S WALL
Vindolanda

BRITANNIA

LANGOBARDI
CERUSCI

GE

Viroconium
Verulamium
Isca
Camulodunum
Londinium
(London)

RONIA

Roma
stia

na

T

Miles
0   100   200   300

0   100 200 300 400
Kilometers

ROMAN LEGIONS ON THE MARCH

SOLDIERING

IN THE

ANCIENT ROMAN ARMY

Susan Provost Beller

Twenty-First Century Books • Minneapolis

To my newest grandchild, Xavier Patrick

Title page image: Roman soldiers, surrounded by shields and spears, stand outside of a tent. This image is from a first or second century A.D. Roman pavement mosaic.

Twenty-First Century Books
A division of Lerner Publishing Group, Inc.
241 First Avenue North
Minneapolis, MN 55401 U.S.A.

Website address: www.lernerbooks.com

Library of Congress Cataloging-in-Publication Data

Beller, Susan Provost, 1949–
    Roman legions on the march: soldiering in the ancient Roman Army / by Susan Provost Beller.
       p.   cm. — (Soldiers on the battlefront)
    Includes bibliographical references and index.
    ISBN 978-0-8225-6781-3 (lib. bdg. : alk. paper)
    1. Rome—Army—Juvenile literature. 2. Rome—Army—Military life—Juvenile literature.
  I. Title.
  U35.B44 2008
  355.00937—dc22   2006037829

Manufactured in the United States of America
1 2 3 4 5 6 — JR — 13 12 11 10 09 08

Contents

> ❝ **All roads lead to Rome."**
>
> — Proverb

Prologue

The trains run and cars travel where the Roman army marched two thousand years ago. Drivers speed by on *autostradas* in Italy, *autoroutes* in France, *autopistas* in Spain, *autobahns* in Germany, and *motorways* in Great Britain, mostly unaware that they are driving on roads developed by the marching soldiers of ancient Rome. The Romans weren't the first to use these paths. The pathways were the same ones taken by early humans from the time they entered Europe. It was Roman soldiers, the legions, however, who made those paths into the roads. These super-highways by ancient standards connected the parts of their vast empire. The saying "All roads lead to Rome" became literally true.

These same armies built cities with impressive walls, temples, baths, theaters, and amphitheaters. They created aqueducts to bring freshwater to their citizens. When it came time to retire, Roman soldiers settled on the frontiers in Hispania (Spain), Gaul (France), Germania (Germany), Britannia (Great Britain), Asia Minor (Turkey), the Middle East, and northern Africa. They intermarried with the local peoples, effectively guaranteeing that the interests of the Roman Empire would be represented in its farthest corners.

We think of them primarily as fighters—the great conquering legions. But more than any army before or since, they were civilizers rather than occupiers. Their job was to thoroughly Romanize the territory they conquered. This Roman system developed one of the best and most effective armies the world has ever seen—an army that conquered and held territories from Africa to Britain. In addition, it built cities that are still with us in modern times.

CHAPTER ONE

THE CITIZEN ARMY

The story of the Roman army opens in 27 B.C. Octavian, the young nephew of a previous ruler, Julius Caesar, had destroyed all opposition and assumed control of the Roman Empire. The Roman Senate had awarded him the title Augustus, meaning "exalted one." Octavian would be known throughout history by this name. New recruits who entered the Roman legions at this time joined just as Rome was beginning to reach the height of its power.

THE BEGINNING OF ROME

Rome grew from a cluster of huts on the Palatine Hill, a small village in central Italy, sometime around the ninth century B.C. The huts were made of wattle and daub, basically sticks and mud. Early Roman history is hard to separate from its myths. Actual records of the era no longer exist. Even the Roman historian Titus Livius (Livy), writing during the reign of Augustus, found most of the information about early Rome "as being suitable rather to the fictions of poetry than to the genuine records of history."

Romulus and Remus, twin brothers descended from Aeneas—a legendary hero of the Trojan War—are the supposed founders of the city. The myth states that they were abandoned near the Tiber River, which winds southward from central Italy. Legend says a female wolf found them and suckled them (fed them milk). Growing to adulthood, they quarreled about where they should build their city. In the fight, Romulus killed Remus and made himself the first king of the city-state of Rome in 753 B.C. The peoples of Rome were known as the Latins, and their region was called Latium. Latium was controlled by the city-state of Etruria, home of the Etruscans, another group that had settled in central Italy. Etruria chose Latium's kings.

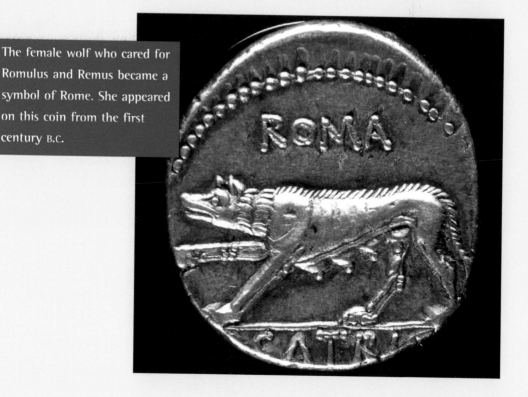

The female wolf who cared for Romulus and Remus became a symbol of Rome. She appeared on this coin from the first century B.C.

FINDING OUT ABOUT THE ROMANS

When something happens in the modern world, a person can turn to library books, newspapers, and the Internet to find information about it. Bloggers analyze just about every topic. So much information is available that it is impossible to read everything about a topic.

But a researcher checking into events in history finds that, farther back in time, information becomes less and less available. The Romans are actually extremely well documented, considering that their empire was at its peak two thousand years ago. However, in comparison to more recent events, we actually have very little information about them.

Historians have to sift through the little bits they have to try to construct the story of Rome's past. It is easiest to research the most important people. The Roman general Julius Caesar, for example, left writings on his campaign in Gaul, and they provide an excellent source on that one event. Emperor Augustus left a short written account of his accomplishments, which became available after his death. That also gives historians some information.

Very few of the sources that do exist were written during the period of the development of the legions. Historians depend on a manual on the Roman army written by Flavius Vegetius. His work helps us to understand the recruitment, training, and tactics of that great military force. But Vegetius's account wasn't written until A.D. 390, when the Roman army was no longer the powerful force it had been in the early years of the empire.

Worse still for historians is that the few existing sources are about a very few Romans—those who were emperors or great generals. The everyday lives of

THE MILITIA

Under the rule of these kings, Rome's military was a citizen militia, a temporary army serving as needed to protect the borders of the city-state. Armies of that time were made up of local landowners. These were the people who would be willing to die to protect their

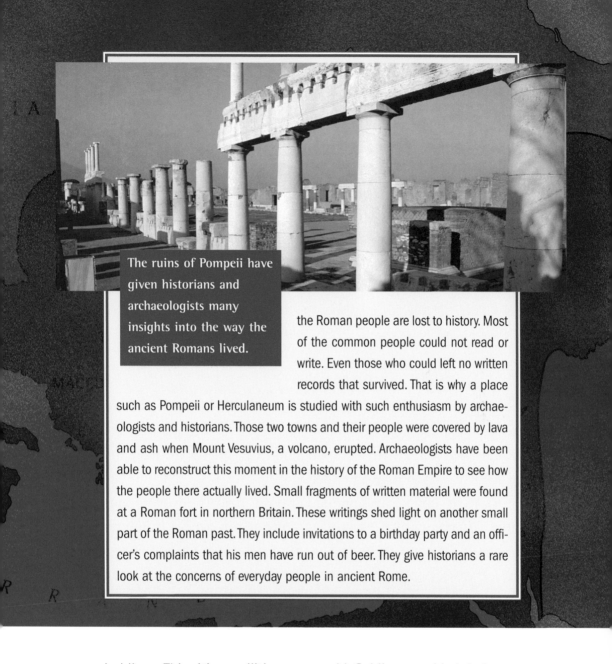

The ruins of Pompeii have given historians and archaeologists many insights into the way the ancient Romans lived.

the Roman people are lost to history. Most of the common people could not read or write. Even those who could left no written records that survived. That is why a place such as Pompeii or Herculaneum is studied with such enthusiasm by archaeologists and historians. Those two towns and their people were covered by lava and ash when Mount Vesuvius, a volcano, erupted. Archaeologists have been able to reconstruct this moment in the history of the Roman Empire to see how the people there actually lived. Small fragments of written material were found at a Roman fort in northern Britain. These writings shed light on another small part of the Roman past. They include invitations to a birthday party and an officer's complaints that his men have run out of beer. They give historians a rare look at the concerns of everyday people in ancient Rome.

holdings. This citizen militia was unpaid. Soldiers provided their own weapons and supplies—another reason poorer, landless men could not enter military service. A citizen militia needed to be a short-term army because the farmer-soldiers had their farms to tend to at home. At any given time, the Roman citizen army had about six thousand foot soldiers (infantrymen) and six hundred cavalrymen and their horses. After their campaigns were completed, they divided the spoils taken from their enemies and returned home. They celebrated these victories with triumphal parades and festivities.

In 509 B.C., a group of Roman nobles overthrew the eighth king of Rome, Tarquin the Proud, and declared Rome a republic, free of Etruscan control. As a republic, Rome was ruled by magistrates who served one-year terms and by the Senate, which was made up of members of the wealthy landowning class known as patricians. The patricians and the equestrian classes (smaller landowners) served as the soldiers of the citizen army. The lower classes of society, called plebeians, were still banned from military service.

THE ARMY OF THE REPUBLIC

By the fourth century B.C., the Romans had expanded into the surrounding areas. They founded the city of Ostia on the Mediterranean Sea. With a seaport, Rome could develop a navy and increase its wealth through trade.

From its earliest days, Rome borrowed freely from other cultures. In one example, the citizen army added javelins (throwing spears) to its equipment after seeing how effectively the Greeks used this weapon in their battles. Rome used knowledge learned from the Etruscans and Greeks to conquer the territory held by both of these peoples.

Within three hundred years of becoming independent of the Etruscans, Rome dominated the entire peninsula of Italy. Expansion of its territories governed Roman military strategy for several hundred years. Rome defended itself by expanding. It used even the threat of an attack as an excuse to take over enemy lands. The Romans had no sense of final borders. They moved ever outward as

These Greek warriors hold javelins and shields. The ancient Romans would later borrow the use of javelins in warfare from the Greeks.

they saw new threats to their country. One modern historian notes that Rome "acquired an empire without really meaning to do so ... for the negative reason that [it] was afraid to see any other nation in that role."

The conquered territories became part of Rome, and some of the conquered peoples, over time, were granted Roman citizenship. The Romans felt they were civilizing these people as well as conquering them. Civilizing meant that the conquered people adopted Roman culture. They spoke the same language (Latin), shared the same customs, and worshiped the same gods as the Romans. They enjoyed all the rights, privileges, and responsibilities of all Romans before them. This concept gave the Romans control of most of the world as they knew it over the next several hundred years.

The Beginnings of an Empire

With Italy under Roman control, the next step was conquest of the lands around the Mediterranean Sea. The city-state of Carthage in present-day Tunisia controlled the Mediterranean at that time. Carthage had been doing exactly what Rome had been doing: acquiring territories and expanding outward. Carthage had become a trading power with a strong navy and a powerful army.

Carthage controlled the island of Sicily, close to southern Italy. A local dispute there in 260 B.C. brought the two powers into direct conflict. A series of small skirmishes led to larger and larger battles. It quickly became apparent that Rome could win on land, but Carthage, with control of the sea, couldn't be defeated. After more than twenty years of fighting between the two powers, Carthage finally gave up. What came to be called the First Punic War (264–241 B.C.) was over. Rome was victorious, but Carthage remained a threat.

One Carthaginian general, Hamilcar Barca, refused to accept the Roman victory. He conquered Spain for Carthage. That conquest provided him with a base of operations closer to Rome. His son Hannibal, whom he trained and molded into a great general, led the fight to destroy Rome. Hannibal's attacks began the Second Punic War (218–202 B.C.). His successful strategy and tactics handed the Romans defeat after defeat. In 216 B.C., the two armies met at Cannae in central Italy. Hannibal inflicted the worst defeat the Romans ever experienced. Rome refused to ask for peace, however. More Roman legions were formed to stop Hannibal's advance. Hannibal had won a number of battles, but he did not have the forces needed to subdue the Romans completely.

The conflict dragged on. In 204 B.C., Roman general Scipio convinced the Senate that an attack should be made on Carthage itself.

Such an attack would force Hannibal to return to defend his homeland. The armies of the two generals met in battle in 202 B.C. at Zama in northern Africa. The Carthaginians were soundly defeated. The Second Punic War ended, and Rome acquired all of Carthage's empire. In the Third Punic War (149–146 B.C.), Carthage again tried to expand into Roman territory. That war ended with the complete destruction of Carthage. After the war, Rome controlled all of Sicily and parts of Spain and northern Africa. One modern historian observed, "Before the wars with Carthage Rome was an Italian power; at the close of them, she was a world power."

At the battle at Zama in 202 B.C., the Roman army led by Scipio defeated the Cathaginian army led by Hannibal. Scipio had a strategy to deal with Hannibal's war elephants. In addition, the Roman cavalry and infantry were better trained than the Carthaginian troops.

Maintaining Roman power had become too big a job for an army of landowners, who could spare only a few years of military service. Removing Roman citizens from their land to defend distant borders was no longer reasonable. Rome needed something that worked better—the world's first professional army.

Marius's Mules

The man who devised and implemented a new permanent, professional army was Gaius Marius. Roman historian Velleius Paterculus called him "a man of rustic birth, rough and uncouth ... a man of unbounded ambition, insatiable, without self-control, and always an element of unrest." Marius was born around 157 B.C. in a small town in the countryside outside of Rome. He came from a family of equestrian rank, the small landowners who were not eligible to be in the Senate. Marius used his fine record of military service to get himself noticed by the ruling class. Then he married into the patrician Julii family to increase his status. Using the power of his new family's connections, he arranged to be named the commander of all Rome's legions stationed in Africa.

Arriving to take over command, he immediately confronted the problems of the overextended citizen army. There was no longer a large enough landowning population for the number of new recruits that were needed. Marius had a solution: "Contrary to law and custom," [observed one historian] "he enlisted many a poor and insignificant man" instead of those "whose property assessment made them worthy to receive [arms]." Roman landowners still provided the officer corps of the new army, but increasingly the ranks would be filled by the poorer citizens of Rome and noncitizens.

Marius did not stop there. He changed every aspect of the soldier's existence, from weapons and food to training and discipline to

This illustration from the early twentieth century shows Roman general Gaius Marius on horseback. Armored troops surround him.

the formations of the soldiers in battle. He took his new recruits and turned them into a fighting force that was unrivaled at the time. Marius demanded performance well beyond that of the citizen army. His training involved long marches to build up physical endurance. His soldiers were expected to carry their own supplies. They learned to prepare their own food too. These requirements earned his soldiers the nickname Marius's Mules, but it meant that Marius could move his well-disciplined legions quickly without waiting for supply wagons to catch up.

A Professional Worth His Salt

Marius made another change that had a major impact on the creation of a professional army. The soldiers he recruited could not afford to equip themselves. Marius's innovation was to give them a salary. Roman soldiers always shared in the bounty of campaigns, each getting their portion of whatever spoils were taken from the conquered enemy. This arrangement was fine if you could afford to support yourself until the campaign was over. But Marius's recruits were not all wealthy. The salary allowed them to enlist and support themselves while waiting to get a share of that bounty.

The legions were paid partly in money and partly in salt, an expensive and necessary item in their diets. In fact, the origin of the word *soldier* is the Latin *sal dare*, which means "to give salt." The Latin word for the salt rations given to the legions was *salarium*, which became the basis for the English word *salary*. The phrase "not worth his salt" is an insult from Roman times.

Marius's Mules enlisted to serve for a long period of time (the length of service varied, usually from twenty to twenty-five years). Those who were Roman citizens received a share of the valuables taken from the people they conquered in addition to their regular pay. At retirement they also received land. By tradition, only Roman citizens were allowed to serve in the Roman legions. However, Marius created a place for those peoples conquered by Rome. Noncitizens could enroll in the auxiliaries to the legions. Auxiliaries (from the Latin word for helper) supplemented the work of the Roman legions. Auxiliaries were trained in specialized skills, such as archery, to be used to support the Roman foot soldiers when they went into battle. The pay was less and their share of the spoils smaller, but they were awarded full Roman citizenship at retirement.

Marius, most likely unintentionally, had created a force for economic advancement that had not existed earlier in the ancient world. A poor man could enlist in the army, work his way through the ranks, and retire with some savings and property.

The poor were grateful for the opportunity the army afforded them, and they joined eagerly. Despite the strict discipline, the harsh training, and service as Marius's Mules, the soldiers were devoted to their commander. It was not surprising that the soldiers lost their ties to home after years of service in the field. The legion became their family. Their commander became their father.

Emperor Augustus, upon gaining control of the empire some years later, refined and codified all army regulations. He made permanent the changes that Marius had instituted around 100 B.C. Marius had given Augustus the tool he needed to expand and govern his empire.

> **"Alert eyes, straight neck, broad chest, muscular shoulders, strong arms."**
>
> —Vegetius, A.D. 390, describing a Roman recruit

CHAPTER TWO

BECOMING A SOLDIER

"If you study carefully the organization of the Roman army, you will realize that they possess their great empire as a reward for valor, not as a gift of fortune." The writer of these words, the Jewish author Josephus, was paying tribute to an enemy. The Romans had defeated the Jews of Palestine when they revolted against Roman rule from A.D. 66 to 70. His respect for the power of this well-trained enemy was no different from that of the other peoples defeated by the power of the legions.

The Roman legions employed hundreds of thousands of men, far more than any other enterprise in the empire. Simply maintaining the army was an organizational challenge of a size and scope previously unknown in history. A similar army—with about the same size and range of operations—would not appear for another fourteen hundred years, during the Napoleonic Wars (1799–1815).

A Soldier in Training

Recruitment took place throughout the empire. To serve in the legions, one had to be a Roman citizen. Roman subjects who were not citizens were recruited for the auxiliary. Vegetius, a Roman military writer during the later Roman Empire, specified that young men were the best choice, especially those from rural rather than urban areas. He thought they tended to be stronger and healthier.

WITH YOUR SHIELD OR ON IT!

The Roman Empire, especially at its most powerful, had a very strong warrior culture. Military service among the wealthy patricians was seen as a normal part of training to be political leaders. Of course, most of the soldiers doing the fighting were not from the patrician classes. Officers, however, tended to be. Caesar came to power through the military. Augustus fought and defeated several other rivals to become emperor. Later emperors were often generals whose troops chose them for the highest office.

As part of this warrior culture, the Romans used a motto that went back to the time of the Spartans, a very militaristic people from Greece. The story is told that Spartan mothers, sending their sons off to war, always told them to "Return with your shield or on it." Bringing back his shield would show that a soldier had either been victorious or at least had not dropped his heavy shield and run from battle. Returning on it meant that he had died a noble death in battle.

The saying was about courage and bravery. But it also showed that all Spartan society, even the mothers, supported having their sons go off to war. Roman women adopted that same philosophy for their own sons, expecting them to serve in the military. This culture was very common during the years of the Roman Republic and in the early years of the Roman Empire. Over the next several hundred years, however, patrician Romans became less willing to send their own sons off to war. Military service was no longer seen as desirable among the upper class. Some historians think that when mothers stopped believing that their sons should return with their shields or on them, the Roman Empire was doomed to fall.

He advised that they should have "alert eyes, straight neck, broad chest, muscular shoulders, strong arms."

The new recruits often provided letters of recommendation when they applied for service. After acceptance, the soldiers were on probation until they successfully completed the equivalent of basic training. Before a recruit could officially join the army, he had to swear an oath of obedience and loyalty to the emperor, called a *sacramentum*.

Vegetius's manual called for intensive training of the recruits. This training was designed in part to increase their strength. It included plenty of running, jumping, swimming, and carrying heavy loads. They also trained in the use of weapons. Vegetius recommended "round wickerwork shields, twice as heavy as those of service weight, and...wooden staves [slats] instead of swords, and these again were double weight." Practicing with the heavier equipment made the regular-weight weapons seem lighter and easier to handle in battle.

With their basic training complete, the recruits faced more specialized training. Tactical training was about more than just the skills needed to fight. It made each individual soldier function as part of a team. Roman soldiers learned to march together in unison. They needed special training in using their weapons safely while fighting in tight military formations. The troops also learned discipline—to follow orders without question—and loyalty to their new profession.

Good discipline instilled in a new recruit carried through when he became part of a legion. Discipline was enforced with severe penalties. The most usual punishment was flogging (whipping). Effective training made penalties unnecessary. A well-trained soldier had such a sense of duty that he would never desert, mutiny (revolt against his superiors), or refuse to obey his officers.

DECIMATION— THE ULTIMATE DISCIPLINE

People who hear about the Roman army and its emphasis on harsh discipline are often horrified at the most severe punishment an army unit could suffer—decimation. The word comes from the Latin word *decem* (number ten).

When a unit had totally disgraced itself, its commander could order that every tenth soldier be killed as a punishment for the entire unit. The soldiers divided into groups of ten and then drew lots. This way, the choice of who was executed was completely random. The selected soldiers were stoned or clubbed to death by the others. Decimation was reserved for only the most terrible of army crimes, such as mutiny, desertion from an assigned post in battle, or dereliction of duty (neglecting to do what was ordered).

Decimation was such a horrible punishment that it was rarely ever needed. In fact, history documents only three occasions on which this punishment was inflicted. One was in 72 B.C. A slave army of 120,000, led by Spartacus, managed to defeat two Roman legions. The legions' new commander, Marcus Crassus, ordered decimation in one cohort (about five hundred men). Most of the time, though, just the thought of decimation was enough to convince soldiers to keep their oaths to the emperor.

A more common punishment was a death sentence for individual soldiers who committed similar failures. Here again, the penalties were stoning or clubbing to death. The death sentence was carried out by fellow soldiers. In theory this was because the condemned soldier's actions had put them all at risk. It also served to deter the others from even considering similar actions.

THE DAY-TO-DAY LIFE OF A SOLDIER

With early training completed, the new legionary (the name for a fully trained Roman soldier) moved on to his normal day-to-day duties, though training would be part of his life until retirement. The Roman army did not fight often. Most of a soldier's career was served in peacetime. And, as one historian notes, "activity and the dull routine of protecting the borders and maintaining the camp were the rule, rather than conflict." The same historian observed that the new soldier might actually find himself doing "the same work he had previously done as a civilian, with very little difference to his way of life."

As the builders and engineers of the Roman Empire, the legions required skilled as well as unskilled labor. The soldier who had a trade as a civilian—for example as a carpenter or a mason (brick layers or stone layer)—was most welcome as a recruit. His skill was useful to the army throughout his military career.

This stone relief from Trajan's column in Rome, Italy, shows soldiers building fortifications. Soldiers who brought skills to the army were highly valued.

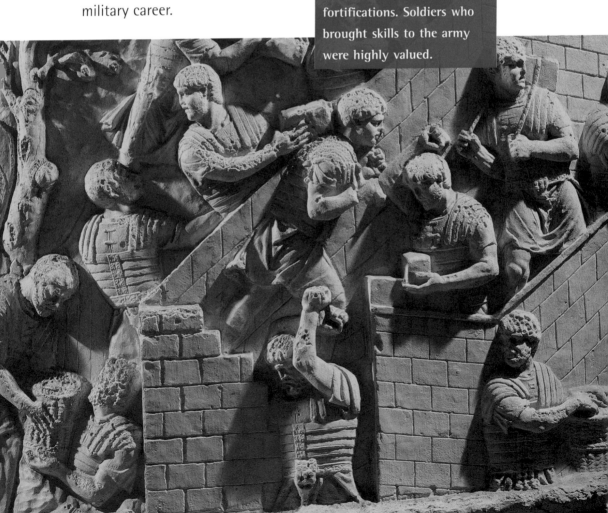

Legionaries were encouraged to learn a trade if they did not already have one. This system filled the needs of the army for skilled workers and provided the soldier with training he could use in civilian life when he retired.

To increase the incentive to learn a skill, those soldiers who did so could reach a rank called *immunis*. This rank brought higher pay and immunity (the privilege of skipping the most unpleasant jobs). All common soldiers were expected to develop wide-ranging skills. Notes one historian, "Every soldier was also an engineer, and the legion built roads, walls, bridges, theaters, and ships. They mined silver and gold, dug canals, and manufactured not only weapons but also pottery, shoes, and other needed items." Each section of the Roman army was designed to be self-sufficient, not tied to a supply train from Rome.

Food

The Roman army may also have been one of the best-fed armies in history. The legions emphasized healthy bodies. Good food was seen as an important factor in meeting that goal. Roman organization made sure that the legions were supplied with this food. A soldier's regular rations consisted of wheat made into porridge or various kinds of bread, as well as meat, olive oil, and wine.

Under the reforms of Marius, the soldiers were responsible for their own cooking. How the food was prepared depended on the day's schedule. If the men knew they would be marching for long hours, for example, their wheat ration would be baked into a flat bread or hard cracker that was easy to eat on the march. Troops stationed in forts could have more variety in their diets. They might have fresh vegetables and fruit and locally caught fish. Costs for food were deducted from the soldier's salary. The soldier, of course, ate what the army provided, and the amount taken from pay was the same for all.

HEALTH CARE FOR THE SOLDIERS

The Romans also placed a strong emphasis on cleanliness and good sanitation. Cleanliness reduces germs, but the germ concept was not understood until the late 1800s. The Romans, with their stress on hygiene kept their soldiers from the most common camp diseases long before scientists would discover why cleanliness was good. Vegetius's manual also stressed the importance of having a good supply of pure water. He observed that it was one of the best ways of keeping troops healthy.

Legionaries wounded in battle received the finest medical treatment available. Each legion carried medical supplies. A physician

This stone carving from A.D. 100 shows a Roman physician next to a medicine cabinet.

and medics were on staff for each cohort (about five hundred men), and the soldiers were trained in first aid. The Roman historian Tacitus emphasized the importance placed on the care of wounded soldiers when he told the story of Agrippina, wife of a Roman general and granddaughter of the emperor Augustus. She "dispensed clothes to needy soldiers, and dressed the wounded."

The Roman army was an impressive organizational machine. After Rome was conquered and the were legions disbanded, no army until modern times would match the Roman emphasis on caring for its soldiers. It was an emphasis that paid off for Roman military leaders. All that training and organization led to an equally impressive result when the army marched into battle.

> "One would not be wrong in saying that their maneuvers are like bloodless battles, and their battles bloodstained maneuvers."
>
> —Josephus, ca. A.D. 75, describing the Roman army

CHAPTER THREE

UNIFORMS AND WEAPONS

Roman soldiers most often fought armies that weren't trained to fight with discipline or as organized units. Rome's enemies also did not have the weapons that were available to the Roman military. They did not wear uniforms. When the Romans went into battle, they deliberately presented a daunting picture of ranked men in splendid uniforms. Often their presence alone could prevent a battle.

DRESSING FOR BATTLE

Although equipment and clothing varied over the years of the empire, a Roman soldier dressed for battle wore a woolen tunic as a first layer. Over this tunic, he wore metal armor that covered his chest. The earliest armor was made of chain mail (interlocked metal rings) but

This Roman breastplate, or cuirass, was made in the 300s B.C. in Italy.

gradually it evolved into a covering made up of armor plates. In addition to his chest armor—called a cuirass—the soldier might have worn metal arm guards (if he was an archer) or leg protectors—called greaves—on his shins. Around his waist he wore a cingulum. This belt supported a sort of apron of leather strips studded with metal. It offered some protection to his lower body in battle and was flexible enough not to hinder movement. On his feet, he wore leather military sandals with soles studded with metal. These sandals were called *caligae*. Archaeological digs at Vindolanda, a fort in northern England, have turned up large numbers of these Roman legionary shoes.

Over his uniform, the legionary wore a red cloak that protected him from the rain and cold. On his head, he wore a metal helmet to protect him from enemy weapons. The helmet had a small ridge on the front to deflect blows to his face. A large extension in the back protected the soldier's neck from slashing sword attacks.

ROMANS IN DRESSES

The everyday dress of all ancient Roman men was a woolen tunic. A tunic is a sleeveless or short-sleeved dress that ends at the knees. Italy has a warm climate.

A sleeveless tunic was comfortable during the hot summer. A loincloth knotted at the side served as underwear. Roman women wore tunics also, but theirs reached their ankles.

In cool weather, a man wealthy enough to have more than one tunic might wear one with longer sleeves. He might also wear a toga over it. A toga is a long cloth wrapped and draped around the body. As it became colder, a person would layer on more tunics. Emperor Augustus supposedly always wore four tunic layers to warm him as he aged and was more sensitive to cold.

When a man went off to war in the citizen army, he wore the same clothing as he had in civilian life. When the army became standardized, the uniform was still a tunic. It was only later that someone designed breeches or short pants to be worn under the tunic. Soldiers did not have to layer their tunics to stay warm. The short red cloak worn over the full uniform provided warmth and protection from the weather.

Rich Roman men who were not soldiers, such as the one pictured in this statue, typically wore togas over tunics.

Kilometers

Soldiers in the auxiliary units generally wore less armor than the legionaries, and their equipment was of a lesser quality. Many auxiliary soldiers were weapons specialists such as archers and slingers (slingshot experts). They were placed in battle formation where their weapons would be most effective against the enemy.

ARMED FOR BATTLE

The legionary soldier was responsible for paying for his own weapons and equipment. Paying for them would make him take better care of them. When he reached retirement age, the soldier returned his equipment to his unit and was repaid for what it had cost him. If he died while in the legions, his unit still bought back the equipment.

On the march, the legionary carried everything with him. Historians give various numbers for the amount of weight the soldier had to carry, some saying as low as 40 pounds (18 kilograms), some as high as 90 pounds (40 kg). Historian Dyan Blacklock chose a middle number. She writes, "Weighing around 66 pounds [30 kg], this gear could include shovels and stakes as well as rations, cooking equipment, and clothing." One gallon (3.75 liters) of milk weighs just over 8 pounds (3 kg), so these soldiers were regularly marching with the weight of about 8 gallons (30 l) of milk on their backs.

Among the items they carried were personal weapons such as the *pilum* (plural *pila*). These were long lances or javelins described by Vegetius as "having thin, triangular heads [that] ... once lodged in a shield could not be broken off and, when thrown skillfully and with force, might easily pierce a cuirass." The point of the lance bent as it pierced a

> "[A pilum] when thrown skillfully and with force, might easily pierce a cuirass."
>
> —Vegetius, A.D. 390

shield, so it could not easily be removed. The enemy soldier would have to abandon his shield, which had become heavy and unwieldy because of the embedded lance. Each soldier carried two pila, one light one for throwing long distances and one heavy one for throwing closer to the enemy line.

The soldier also carried a dagger, called a *pugio*, and a short sword, called a *gladius* (plural *gladii*). In battle the soldier threw his pilum as he charged at the enemy and then fought with his

A typical Roman soldier wore a breastplate, a helmet, a cingulum, and sandals. He carried a scutum, a pilum, and a gladius.

gladius once close contact was made. The dagger and sword were based on Spanish weapons that the legionaries had seen used against them when they conquered Hispania. The sword was especially deadly against the troops of tribes who did not wear armor in battle.

The legionary also carried a large shield called a scutum. A Roman soldier was taught to force his shield against an enemy to restrict his movement. Then the Roman soldier could thrust his sword into a vulnerable part of the enemy soldier's body, such as his abdomen. A sword thrust was more likely to cause a mortal wound than a slashing sword blow. Most enemy deaths in battle were caused by the legionaries' skillful use of their gladii in close combat.

TACTICS

A battle might be fought with several legions under the control of one commander. The makeup of the legions varied over the years. But as a rule, the legionary soldier was first part of a *contubernium*, a group of eight men who shared a tent or barracks. Ten of these groups (80 men) made a century and were led by a centurion. Six centuries (480 men) made a cohort. Ten cohorts (4,800 men) made a *legio*, or legion.

Usually Roman generals used the regular legions primarily as heavy infantry troops in massed attacks. Infantry soldiers were the core of the legion, but each legion also had a small cavalry unit of about 120 men attached to it.

The cavalry was known as the *equitatus*, from the Latin for "horse." The auxiliaries provided most of the cavalry troops for the legions. These mounted auxiliaries were mostly archers who served as scouts for the regular legions. The cavalry also patrolled areas around the massed troops and protected the movements of the legions on the march.

This bronze figurine of an eagle standard bearer from the first century A.D. symbolized power in the ancient Roman world.

In addition each legion had general officers, a paymaster, medical personnel, and a person who carried the eagle or standard (symbol) of the legion. It was a special honor to be the standard bearer. Each legion took great pride in defending its eagle.

When the legions went into battle, every soldier knew his role and where he belonged. The Romans approached battle the way they approached everything else in the military—with careful planning. Josephus provided the best description of the mighty Roman military machine, one that is quoted often. He said of them, "One would not be wrong in saying that their maneuvers are like bloodless battles, and their battles bloodstained maneuvers."

SPECIAL WEAPONS

In many battles, only the normal weapons carried by the soldiers came into play. The javelins and swords of the legionaries and the bows and arrows of the auxiliary were generally enough to stop the attack of a charging enemy force.

In other battles, especially sieges when they surrounded a fortified city, the Roman army used more complex weapons. Battering rams—made of wood and covered with iron tips—called *aries*, knocked down walls. The Romans took the battering ram one step further. They covered it with "a housing built of sturdy timbers rather like a hut on wheels." This provided protection for the soldiers using it, according to military historian Peter Connolly. The Romans also had two kinds of catapults. These wooden machines used ropes and counterweights to throw projectiles farther and more accurately than a person could. One of their catapults (a *ballista*) threw stones and the other (a *catapulta*) was like a huge crossbow for firing arrows. They also created movable siege towers to reach the tops of fortification walls.

Roman soldiers man a ballista that is about to launch a stone. The ballista was built into a siege tower during Julius Caesar's campaign in Gaul (France) in 52 B.C.

At Masada, in modern-day Israel, the Roman army built a massive ramp 100 yards (91 meters) high, about as tall as a modern football field is long, to reach a besieged Jewish settlement on a cliff. The Jewish historian Josephus described the attack from the ramp. On it, "a tower was erected . . . and entirely covered with iron plates from which the Romans, with missile volleys from many quick-firers and *ballistae*, drove off the defenders on the ramparts and forced them to keep under cover." The ramp was an amazing piece of engineering and can still be seen by visitors to Masada.

THE MISSING ROMAN NAVY

Modern military power covers land, sea, and air. The United States, like other powerful nations, has an army that fights on land, a navy that controls the seas (with a marine corps that deploys from navy ships), and an air force. The air force is a recent phenomenon, of course, so one would not expect to find an air force in the ancient world. But with the size of the Roman Empire, one would expect to find a navy.

Rome put all her military efforts into infantry. Generals planned on troops marching to battle and fighting on foot. Other battle functions could be performed by auxiliary troops, but those functions (such as archery and cavalry) were seen as secondary (therefore auxiliary) to the main strategies and tactics of the legions.

The navy suffered a similar lack of respect. Rome had fielded a navy during the time of the republic when the country was at war with Carthage. Once the Punic Wars ended and Rome controlled the Mediterranean, the navy quietly faded into insignificance. The triremes and other oared boats that had been needed to destroy Carthage had no place in the tactics of the legions.

Ships were still built and used for moving legions to places such as Britain. But they were ships for transport, not warships for conquest. The last major sea battle of the ancient world was the Battle of Actium in 31 B.C., in which Octavian, soon to be known as the emperor Augustus, defeated his rival Mark Antony.

Most battles that the legions took part in were far from Rome. The emperors were quite happy to have the powerful legions fighting far away, where they would be no threat at home. Often the legionaries received gifts of money from incoming emperors, which were actually bribes to ensure their support.

Emperors could justify keeping the legions in the field because they had their own military force stationed in Rome. This force was known as the Praetorian Guard. The guard members were "the envy of the legionaries stationed at the frontiers," according to one historian. They lived in Rome in more comfortable conditions than did the army in the field. They received better pay and were allowed to retire after fewer years of service. Serving as personal bodyguards of the emperors, they sometimes meddled in the government. In one case, several disgruntled members of the Praetorian Guard assassinated Emperor Caligula. They threatened to use force if their choice of emperor didn't succeed him. With the power and skills the legions possessed, it is no wonder that emperors sent them elsewhere.

"I send you a warm invitation to come to us on September 11th for my birthday celebrations, to make my day more enjoyable by your presence."

—Claudia Severa, wife of Aelius Brocchus, ca. A.D. 103 writing from a Roman army fort

CHAPTER FOUR

THE ROMAN CAMP

In 1901 Ransom E. Olds invented the assembly line. Henry Ford modified it by adding conveyor belts for the manufacture of the first mass-produced automobiles. But the concept of reproducing the same item consistently and quickly can be traced back to the Roman army. It reproduced a whole camp. The camp was either a *castra*, which was built on the march, or a fort, if the army would be staying in one place for a while. The legionaries, historian Adrian Goldsworthy noted, "advanced slowly and cautiously, and at the end of each day's march . . . constructed a large camp, identical to the ones it had built, and would continue to build, on every other night of the march."

A NEW CAMP EVERY NIGHT

Building a camp or fort may not sound like the greatest of achievements. Other peoples before the Romans had built earth and wood fortresses, mostly on the tops of hills, to defend themselves from attacking enemies. The Romans, however, built whole fortified camps every night while on the march. For longer-term stays, they built fortresses of stone. Building so many camps and forts forced them to develop an organized system. Every camp and fort was built according to the same plan. Every soldier had a role to play so that the camp could be built quickly. The last thing a commander needed was to be making new decisions every day on the location of the latrines (public bathrooms), for example.

No remains of short-term Roman camps exist, since the camps were built of wood that has long since decayed. But stone forts can be found

This reconstruction of a Roman wooden fort shows what the defenses might have looked like during the first century B.C. The main wall would have been built each night. The towers were only built for long stays, such as sieges.

wherever the Romans were stationed during their long years of conquest. Sometimes only bits remain, especially in places where cities were later built on the sites. The sites and their forts varied in size, depending on the needs of the commander and the number of troops, but the same plans were used throughout the empire. A fort named Segontium in Caernarvon in northern Wales was laid out just like the fort Segedunum at Wallsend in northern England near the Scottish border.

These two forts look much like others in Britain, such as Vercovicium (in Housesteads), Cilurnum (in Chester), and Vindolanda or Isca (in Caerleon, Wales). It's not surprising that a similarity exists among all the Roman forts in Britannia, since they were built over a

Britain holds the remains of many Roman stone forts. These remains of a Roman barracks are in Caerleon, Wales.

The ruins of Roman forts can be found throughout the countries that once made up the Roman world. These ruins are next to Lake Nasser in Nubia, Egypt.

relatively short period. However, this pattern was followed throughout the Roman Empire. Modern visitors can see examples of the same design in places such as Saalburg, Germany, and in the deserts of Egypt and Algeria.

How to Build a Camp

The camps built for a single night's use were simple affairs. The chief surveyor of a legion on the march traveled ahead of the soldiers and selected the best location for that night's stop. He looked for an open space that was near water. A site on a flat hill would provide a good view of the surrounding area to protect the camp from surprise attack. When the legionaries arrived at the site, they immediately began to dig a deep trench around the edge of it. They piled the dirt they dug in a mound at the inside of the trench. The Roman military writer Vegetius noted that the depth of the ditch depended on whether the army was in hostile territory or not. It might be as much as 9 feet (3 m) deep and 12 feet (4 m) wide. The mound formed a raised rampart, a wall of dirt surrounding the camp that an enemy would have to climb in order to attack. Each legionary on the march carried with him two long wooden stakes. He embedded these stakes into the freshly built rampart, creating a protective wall. The soldiers pitched their tents inside the wall.

All camps were built on the same plan, with only minor variations to account for differences in terrain. Each unit knew where to erect its tents each night in the camp's enclosed rectangle. The camp looked like a miniature town with streets and fortified exits that were closely guarded. In the morning, when the bugle blew, the legionaries packed up their tents, grabbed two stakes from the ramparts, and marched to the next location. There the process began again.

This arrangement had an impact on how long and far the legionaries could march in a day. Historian Albert Harkness, describing one Roman campaign, said that the march "began at four or five o'clock in the morning and continued till about midday. Most of the afternoon was occupied in fortifying the camp." Because of this schedule, he estimated the distance covered by the legionaries to be about 15 miles (24 km) a day.

The pace of the army was usually limited by the need to construct a fortified camp each day. But sometimes an army needed to march farther than that. In the Gallic (French) Campaign, the legions once marched 50 miles (80 km) through the night.

LONG-TERM FORTRESSES

The forts that the legionaries inhabited as long-term camps were also built by the soldiers—this time with stone. First, they quickly constructed a fort of timber to establish control of the area. Then they began the permanent fort of local stone. What they built depended on the circumstances. It could range from a single fort to an entire complex, such as the more than 80 miles (130 km) of Hadrian's Wall in northern England.

Hadrian's Wall is similar to walls built in other parts of the empire. Emperor Hadrian ordered it constructed after visiting Britannia in A.D. 122.

Hadrian's Wall was built to defend the southern part of Britain from raiding northern tribes in the second century A.D.

ROMAN SLAVES

The Roman legions built their own camps and their own roads. Slave labor was not used for these projects. But that does not mean that the Romans had no slaves. Slavery was common in the ancient world. Slaves were used in Egypt and Greece before the time of Rome.

Slavery was an important part of Rome's economy. Roman slaves were bought and sold in an active slave trade. This slavery was not based on race. Slaves generally were conquered peoples, prisoners of war, or the children of the Roman poor. Roman slaves were an expensive investment so their owners usually treated them well and kept them healthy. Sometimes their owners even paid them for their service.

Prisoners of war might be enslaved. But after a term of service, they might very well either be freed by their owners. Since they earned some wages, they might be able to buy their freedom. With freedom came full Roman citizenship and citizenship for their children.

Greek slaves were the most prized because of the high level of education in Greece. They often worked as scribes (writers), accountants, teachers, or doctors. Obviously, these very skilled slaves led an easier life than those working in the countryside as farm laborers. Skilled slaves often were more part of the family than a piece of property. Tiro, the slave of the famous orator Cicero, is said to have edited Cicero's speeches. He wrote manuals on the proper use of Latin and invented a form of shorthand to use in note taking. Cicero freed him, and he worked for Cicero until the orator died.

Within Roman society, the father had ownership of his children and the power of life and death over them. The head of the family had full license to sell into slavery a son who displeased him.

GE

PANNONIA

Roma

Ostia

NORTH AFRICA

Miles
0   100   200   300

0 100 200 300 400
Kilometers

The wall was designed to protect the southern part of Britain, which was mostly under Roman rule, from the raiding tribes in the north. A timber wall was quickly constructed across the narrowest part of the country. Then Roman legionaries went to work to create a more permanent fortification.

Historians believe that local people may have been employed to assist in transporting building materials. But all records indicate that the bulk of the construction was done by the soldiers. Notes one modern guide to Hadrian's Wall: "Within their ranks the legions contained architect-engineers, surveyors, masons, carpenters, and glaziers [glassmakers]—in short all the skills required for even the most massive building task." Historians estimate that this enormous project took about six years. It was probably the work of three Roman legions that had been relocated from Caerleon in Wales, Chester on the northwestern border of Wales, and York in northern England.

Each legion had representatives of all the necessary trades, a Roman policy for the military. So each was able to construct its own section completely, from digging to quarrying stone to building the wall itself and the numerous forts and watchtowers along it. Archaeologists have found stones inscribed with the numbers of the legions, marking their work.

The forts were very functional. Administrative buildings, including a headquarters building, a home for the commandant, and barracks for the soldiers were erected within the walls. Archaeologists can determine from the foundations how many legionaries were stationed at a particular fort, including the number and proportion of infantry and cavalry. The cavalrymen had larger rooms than the foot soldiers, perhaps so that they could store their horses' tack (reins, harnesses, and saddles).

Developing the Area around the Fort

With the fort completed, the legionaries often built other structures as a community grew outside the fort walls. Such a settlement, associated with a fort, was known as a *vicus*, and archaeologists have found them near many Roman forts. For the soldiers, the vicus must have seemed at least a little like the home communities they had left behind when they enlisted. The vicus also made home a little more pleasant for the families of high-ranking Roman officers who were allowed to be married. Although officers could not bring their wives and children on campaigns, they could bring them to live near the long-term camps. Among the interesting finds at Vindolanda, along Hadrian's Wall, was an invitation from one officer's wife to another woman at a camp nearby. She wrote to her friend, Lepidina, "I send you a warm invitation to come to us on September 11th for my birthday celebrations, to make my day more enjoyable by your presence."

This invitation from Claudia Severa to Lepidina found at Vindolanda is one of the earliest known pieces of writing in Latin by a woman.

The presence of a vicus probably depended on how long the fort was occupied. It also depended on how much security the fort provided for the surrounding area. In Spain, where the army had little in the way of military resistance to worry about, the soldiers often set up their own farms, raising crops and grazing sheep and cattle. The Roman general Julius Caesar, according to noted historian Leonard Curchin, worried about the Second Legion which "had served in Spain for so long that they had become hispanised [like the Spanish], acquiring property...and indeed regarding themselves as Spaniards."

This situation was, perhaps, the biggest problem of having an army that was more than a fighting force. An army of builders who could construct a camp on the march and then create sturdy stone forts was an army that would eventually become too settled. It would be difficult to maintain these troops at the level of discipline that had won Rome an empire.

> "[He] leaped down from his horse, stripped off his suit of armour, and seating himself at Caesar's feet remained motionless."
>
> —Plutarch, ca. A.D. 110

CHAPTER FIVE

ROMAN LEGIONS VICTORIOUS

"To me four qualifications seem requisite to form a complete general," wrote the orator Cicero, "a thorough knowledge of war, valour, authority, and good fortune." With the right general, the legions were a powerful weapon for conquest. No one in Roman history fit Cicero's description more perfectly than Gaius Julius Caesar. This general conquered Gaul and then returned home and overthrew the republic. The story of Caesar's conquest of Gaul illustrated what made the legions such a powerful and dangerous force for the empire.

JULIUS CAESAR

Gaius Julius Caesar is certainly the most famous of all Roman generals and perhaps of all Romans. Born into the prominent Julii family on

This statue of Gaius Julius Caesar shows the general dressed in armor.

July 13, 100 B.C., the future general was well educated. Because he was trained in Roman law, he understood the many political intrigues of Rome. It was his daring and brilliance as a commander, however, that would give him victory and allow him to attain Rome's highest offices.

When he was a young man, Caesar traveled to Rhodes, a Greek island, to continue his education. On the way, he was captured by pirates, a common hazard for those who traveled the Mediterranean Sea. Caesar paid the required ransom and was freed. But determined to be avenged, he acquired ships and pursued the pirates, capturing and killing them. It was a bold move that revealed Caesar's toughness and determination. It also served as a good prediction of his future exploits.

Caesar broadened his experience in a series of civilian posts in the provinces and in Rome over the next several years. He learned finance as a quaestor (the supervisor of the treasury) in Baetica, one of the Roman regions of Hispania. He also oversaw public festivals and contests as an aedile, the Roman administrator for public buildings and events in Rome. Elected *pontifex maximus*, or high priest—an administrative post overseeing religious rites—he made himself part of the religious establishment of Rome. He returned to Baetica in Hispania as its governor. There Caesar used some minor revolts in the province as an excuse to capture and plunder several towns.

Next, in Rome, he was appointed one of the two consuls for the year. This shared position was the highest office in the government of the Roman Republic. Caesar, as consul, became a reformer, changing tax policies and opening the record of Senate proceedings to the public. Convinced that he was better suited to governing than the Roman Senate, he took over the government in 60 B.C. He and his friends Crassus and Pompey ruled as a triumvirate, a committee of three.

CONQUERING GAUL

At this time, Gaul was inhabited by an unstable collection of Celtic tribal groups in the areas that became France and Belgium. Gaul was supposedly under the control of Rome, but the Romans there were often under attack by neighboring tribes. In 58 B.C., the triumvirate gave Caesar four legions of soldiers (about twenty thousand men) stationed in Gaul. His task was to subdue the province.

Caesar was the right general for the task. The legions quickly attacked and defeated the Helvetians, a tribal group from present-day Switzerland that was attempting to claim part of Gaul. Because

The Helvetians *(above)* attempted to claim part of Gaul. They became one more tribe that Julius Caesar and the Roman legions conquered in the first century B.C.

of his quick victory, wrote a historian in the introduction to Caesar's own commentaries, "one Gallic people after another presented to the conqueror their protestations of allegiance, while the tidings of victory filled Rome with joy and gladness."

Building on the success of his legions, Caesar planned a much more ambitious campaign. Using rumors that a Belgian tribe, the Remi, was planning an attack, he offered his legions to defend his new Gallic allies. The result was six years of war. Victory by the Roman army was a foregone conclusion. The legions were easily a more skilled fighting force than the tribes they faced, despite often being greatly outnumbered by them. Though victory was inevitable, it would not be easy.

Caesar and his army repeatedly met and defeated various tribes in battle. Even so, attacks on the legions from Celtic tribes that had not been subdued and from the Germanic tribes to the east continued. It was a frustrating fight for the Romans. They easily defeated their disorganized enemy in battle. That enemy, however, would simply slip away and attack again. With enemies that refused to fight by Roman rules, it was inevitable that discipline would break down, even among the well-trained Roman legionaries.

Caesar described one such occasion. Troops panicked when they heard "remarks uttered by Gauls and traders, who affirmed that the Germans were men of a mighty frame and an incredible valour and skill at arms." He said, "So great was the panic and so suddenly did it seize upon all the army, that it affected in serious fashion the intelligence and the courage of all ranks." Caesar responded quickly to the situation, announcing that he would attack immediately, with only one legion if the others would not follow him. The soldiers, shamed by his courage, overcame their fears. They defeated the Germanic tribe they were facing, and the crisis passed.

> "So great was the panic and so suddenly did it seize upon all the army, that it affected in serious fashion the intelligence and the courage of all ranks."
> —Julius Caesar, 58 B.C.

Caesar's personal leadership carried the campaign to victory. One historian noted, "The common soldier is largely what his commander makes him; and under Caesar the Roman soldier was at his best."

WHY THE ROMAN LEGIONS WERE LIKE TURTLES

Pick up a box turtle from the woods, and it will immediately pull its head and legs into its shell. A hard shell is the turtle's successful defense tactic. Some Roman military tactician must have studied turtles, because the best-known military formation of the Roman legions was the testudo, or tortoise *(demonstrated by reenactors below)*.

Roman soldiers carried very large shields made out of thin layers of wood glued together at angles to make them stronger. The center of the front of the shield had a large iron or bronze circle attached to it. The metal of the circle

went through the shield and became a handle on the inside for the soldier to hold. On the outside, it formed a convex bump to deflect weapons that hit it.

Formed into groups of twenty-seven men in four rows, legions presented an impenetrable barrier to incoming spears as they advanced. Most of the front row faced their shields forward, crouching behind them so they were fully protected. The two soldiers on each end turned their shields to the side for protection. The two end men in the next three rows also turned their shields to the side. The interior fifteen men all overlapped their shields above the group, providing full protection, like a turtle's shell, from all but the rear. Moving forward, the testudo was perfectly protected, and the mass of men was said to be dense enough to stop a chariot!

Those soldiers followed him through all of Gaul. They fought fierce opposition in Germany and across the English Channel in the wilds of Britannia before the campaign ended.

VICTORY AT LAST!

The final battle of the campaign in Gaul took place in September 52 B.C. One tribal leader, Vercingetorix, realized that Caesar's strategy was destroying the tribes one by one. He organized over eighty thousand men to resist the Roman troops. They fortified themselves in Alesia, a town in

Julius Caesar and the Roman legions besiege Alesia in 52 B.C. in this sixteenth-century oil painting. The victory gave Rome control of Gaul.

eastern Gaul, probably not far from present-day Dijon. Vercingetorix knew that another army of 240,000, led by his cousin Vercassivellaunus, was coming to his aid. Caesar laid siege to the fortifications of Alesia, building an enormous series of trenches facing the town. He also prepared his troops for the army coming up behind them. Then he sent his cavalry to draw the enemy out of the city and into the open. His strategy worked. Vercingetorix and his troops left their fortifications and were defeated by the Roman legions.

Meanwhile, other Roman legions defended the fortifications against the attack on the rear of the Roman line by Vercassivellaunus. When it looked as though the back line would not hold, Caesar ordered a small group of six thousand legionaries to leave the lines and attack Vercassivellaunus from his rear. The enemy was taken by surprise and panicked. The battle had been brutal, but the Roman army triumphed.

Plutarch described the end as the enemy "finally surrendered. And the leader of the whole war, [Vercingetorix], after putting on his most beautiful armour and decorating his horse, rode out through the gate. He made a circuit round Caesar, who remained seated, and then leaped down from his horse, stripped off his suit of armour, and seating himself at Caesar's feet remained

> "[Vercingetorix] remained motionless, until he was delivered up to be kept in custody for the triumph."
>
> —Plutarch, ca. A.D. 110

motionless, until he was delivered up to be kept in custody for the triumph." Caesar took Vercingetorix to Rome to march in his grand triumphal parade. Then the captive leader was put to death.

Vercingetorix *(left)* rides up on his horse to surrender to Julius Caesar *(seated)*. This painting is from the late nineteenth century.

An estimated one million people, one-third of the population of Gaul, died in the campaign. Another million became slaves. The legions had achieved an overwhelming victory after a long, sustained fight. They had secured for Rome one of its largest provinces.

What Caesar and the legions had accomplished in Gaul was an amazing victory. Caesar had shown how the right general could harness this well-trained and well-disciplined fighting force and use it to conquer vast territories against large enemy forces. With victory his, Caesar illustrated the danger the powerful legions could be to the government of Rome. Taking one of the legions with him, he crossed over the Rubicon River into Italy in 49 B.C. The government in Rome had always kept the legions away from the city. For Caesar to bring the army there was the ultimate defiance. With the legion behind him, Julius Caesar made himself the sole leader of the Roman Empire.

THE POLITICAL GENERAL

By 48 B.C., the Roman Republic had been abolished in all but name. Caesar was appointed dictator for life. This position was not hereditary, so he could not

Caesar *(center, on platform)* speaks to the legions after crossing the Rubicon.

HOW CAESAR GAVE HIS NAME TO KINGS

Upper-class Romans used three names. The first was the equivalent of our own first names. The second was the name of the gens or clan. The third name, called a cognomen, was a further way of identifying people with similar names.

Gaius Julius Caesar is the person known to history as the great Roman general who overthrew the Roman Republic. Some assume Julius is his first name and Caesar is his last. Others assume that his name was Gaius Julius and that Caesar was his title. In fact, he was Gaius of the Julii clan within the Caesar branch.

When Caesar's nephew and heir, Octavian, defeated his enemies in the civil war that took place after Caesar's death, he took the name *Caesar* because he inherited the cognomen from his uncle. The next emperors, through Nero, also inherited this cognomen.

The title *Caesar*—which the later German rulers translated as "kaiser" and the Russians as "czar"—never meant "ruler," "king," or "dictator" before it was Gaius Julius's cognomen. But *kaiser* and *czar* have these meanings in modern times.

officially hand it on to a son or other relative. However, with the powers that he controlled, it would not be difficult to pass on his authority to a successor of his choice. A group of senators plotted to assassinate this new dictator and restore the republic. They wanted to bring control of the legions back to the Senate and the leaders it appointed.

In 44 B.C., the senators succeeded in assassinating Julius Caesar. But his death did not lead to the restoration of the republic. Instead, it led to seventeen years of civil war as differing factions in Rome struggled for power. Caesar's nephew and heir, Octavian, finally emerged as the undisputed leader. Called simply Augustus, he ruled long and successfully. His reign guaranteed that the republic would never return. The Pax Romana (Roman Peace), which he vowed to bring to the Roman world, led the legions to their most active role as warriors and civilizers.

> "Until they had surrendered all they possessed, sacred and profane."
>
> —Livy, 29 B.C.–A.D.17

CHAPTER SIX

THE PAX ROMANA

"Romanization was Rome's genius, and the key to her abiding triumph," wrote one historian. Perhaps the most interesting thing about the Roman conquest was that it was more than a military action. It was not enough to have the victorious legions conquer the known world. The conquered territory had to be held.

CIVILIZING THE BARBARIANS

The Roman leaders saw themselves as the civilizers of the "barbarians" in the world around them. Other nations had conquered in the past. They had brought their knowledge and skills to the people they conquered. Rome, especially at the height of its imperial power, brought Roman ideas of civilization to the outside world. These included improved transportation, communication, and even hygiene. The Pax Romana was the real force that expanded the empire and kept it together.

S.P.Q.R.—THE ROMAN MOTTO THAT LIVES ON

If you walk the streets of modern Rome and look down, you will see the letters S.P.Q.R. on all the manhole covers you cross. Look up as you enter the ruins of the Roman Forum, and the same letters appear on the Arch of Titus. This monument was erected in A.D. 70 to honor the Roman victory in the Jewish-Roman War (66–70).

The letters stand for *Senatus Populusque Romanus*, "the Senate and the Roman People." The phrase first appeared during the years of the Roman Republic. It symbolized the Senate's governing power and its responsibility to represent the people. When Rome became an empire, the letters still marked Roman authority. The Senate had lost much of its power, but all the emperors at least pretended that they ruled by the will of the Senate and served as the spokespersons for the common people. Even with all the changes in the government of Italy over the centuries, these letters are still used as a symbol of its authority.

One historian notes the sequence followed in civilizing the empire, using Hispania as an example. He saw "a colonial policy based at first on military lines," which later formed a civilian government that illustrated "the benefits of Roman rule and Roman customs among the peoples of the province." When the people of the colonies saw the benefits they gained from Roman improvements in daily life, they often wanted to be Romans too.

The Romans were blunter in their description of how they ensured the loyalty of newly conquered peoples. Wrote the Roman historian Livy, "it was the practice of the Romans . . . not to treat such people as pacified nor to exercise authority over them until they had surrendered all they possessed, sacred and profane, and until they, the Romans, had received hostages, taken away their arms, and placed garrisons in their towns." Conquered territories also were required to send some of their children to Rome as hostages to ensure they did not rebel. The policy was quite successful, because the conquered people received advantages from Rome that benefited them in many ways.

OPPORTUNITIES TO BECOME ROMAN

One of the ways Romanization was achieved was that Rome offered the conquered peoples places in the auxiliary troops, the companions to the legions themselves. A veteran who served in the military as an auxiliary would retire, if he survived, as a Roman citizen with all the benefits that came with citizenship. Roman citizenship gave the veteran of the auxiliary an important legal status in society. He could enter into contracts, hold office, marry legally, and have the right to defend himself in a court of law. Through him, his sons had the same benefits. A

The emperor Trajan issued this bronze military diploma in the second century A.D. It granted a Spanish junior officer Roman citizenship and the right to legal marriage.

veteran's son could serve in the legions themselves and make three times as much money as his father made as an auxiliary. Being conquered by Rome meant economic and social opportunities often well beyond those available before conquest.

Though Rome was happy to use the people of its colonies as auxiliary troops, it understood the danger of keeping these trained troops close to their homes. There they might use their training to try to free themselves from Roman rule. The government in Rome developed a policy of moving new recruits away from their homelands, sending them to widely separated areas. Auxiliary units included people from all over the empire within their ranks. For example, historians have documented auxiliary legions in Britannia made up of units from Gaul, Lusitania (in Spain), Thracia (modern-day Turkey and Bulgaria), and Tampiana (modern-day Hungary). A cavalry unit came from Sarmatian (modern-day Ukraine and the Baltic regions). The military family of the soldiers for the next twenty-five years was as varied as the empire itself.

Over time, this system had an impact on the legions. Many retired auxiliary soldiers had sons who automatically became Roman citizens at birth. Those sons, when grown, were eligible to enlist in the legions. Over the centuries, the legions became less and less Italian.

Leaving Its Mark

Even though the legions became less Italian, the empire left a visible mark on the face of the land it ruled. The mark of the Pax Romana is found every place the legions conquered. Barely noticeable mounds mark the earthen Antonine Wall in Scotland. Bridges still carry cars over a river in Alcantara, Spain. The remains of Roman forts and villas are in Germany and Turkey. Several European cities still use amphitheaters and theaters built by the Romans. People can hear a concert under the watchful eye of a statue of the emperor Augustus in a magnificently preserved theater in Orange, France.

Aqueducts built by Roman soldiers still carry water. Other Roman constructions—the Roman baths in Bath, England; the Porta Negra fortified gate in Trier, Germany; and the streets of Leptis Magna in northern Africa—serve as the backdrop for the photographs of thousands of modern-day tourists. Two thousand years after the height of Roman power and about sixteen hundred years after Rome was destroyed, its monuments still draw thousands of visitors in a vast area ranging from Scotland to northern Africa and from Portugal to Iran.

The Roman baths in Bath, England, were built by the Romans over a natural spring that provided the bath with hot water.

AUGUSTUS AND THE FIRST POST OFFICE

The Roman Empire depended on speedy communications. The excellent network of Roman roads helped move people and goods throughout the empire with great efficiency. To carry urgent messages to and from the emperor, a rider on horseback could potentially travel 200 miles (322 km) in one day along the system of Roman roads. Roman historian Suetonius tells us that at the start of his reign, Emperor Augustus maintained a series of runners on foot at various locations along the road system. They could relay messages from one to another so the emperor could communicate with his legions. The system frustrated him because messages took so long to get through.

A great organizer and reformer, Augustus came up with a new system of communications. Postboys (as Suetonius calls them) had access to chariots that carried them and their messages to Rome. The chariots were set up at various posting stations throughout the empire. Changing chariots as needed, a messenger could quickly travel to Rome to deliver a letter. The system allowed the emperor to talk with the messenger to get more information or background on the situation. What Augustus had set up was his own personal postal service.

However, more than Roman architecture came with the legions. Rome was responsible for an increase in educational opportunity throughout the empire. It also brought to the conquered lands a level of hygiene through its baths and health care that would not be matched until modern times.

SHARING THE BEST FROM THROUGHOUT THE EMPIRE

Rome and its legions provided an opportunity for the people and cultures of Europe to mix. Some of this mixing was direct, as veteran soldiers often chose to remain where they had been stationed and to marry locally when they retired. Most exchanges were indirect. Rome sought out the most admirable features in the cultures it conquered and incorporated these features over time into its own culture. Rome then brought these changes to other parts of its empire.

Some say Rome stole a number of ideas, particularly those of the Greeks and Etruscans. On the other hand, Rome passed on to the lands it conquered the ideas, traditions, and cultures it encountered. Roman soldiers adopted the religions of their former enemies, worshiping the Mithras of the Greeks, for example, in underground caves with secret rituals and initiations. People throughout the Roman world enjoyed Greek art, literature, and theater. The Romans borrowed an alphabet from the Etruscans, who had earlier taken it from the Greeks. This alphabet became the basis for all modern-day western European written languages.

There were also the more practical exchanges throughout the empire. The Roman army rid the seas of pirates. This allowed the residents of Britannia to import wines

This stone tablet from the first half of the first cnetury A.D. shows the written Roman language, known as Latin. The Romans used the alphabet of the Etruscans. The inscription is a dedication to Romulus, the legendary founder of Rome.

from Spain without fearing the loss of their ships and goods. All kinds of foods were traded throughout the empire. Pottery from Asia found its way to Britannia. So did art and music.

But, in attempting to bring a single culture to their empire, the Romans actually were responsible for the mixing of cultures and ideas from Britain to Africa and Asia Minor. For example, Emperor Septimius Severus married Julia Domna from Syria. She brought with her several Syrian judges who worked to improve the Roman court system.

Roman roads may have all led to Rome and the central control of the empire may have originated there. Those roads, however, also led from Rome to other places, with other cultures and ideas. Romanization made the Roman world one culture, but it was a culture that rapidly evolved from the original Roman model. Especially in the eastern empire, where well-established civilizations already existed, the conquest brought changes to the conquerors. Rome continued to take Romanization to every land it conquered. Each land, in turn, changed in its own way some aspect of Roman culture itself.

"Kingdom and household alike were plundered like prizes of war . . . his widow Boudicca was flogged."

—Tacitus, ca. A.D. 117

CHAPTER SEVEN

DEFEAT AND THE END OF ROMAN EXPANSION

The story of Roman legionaries is not one of unbroken successes. There were spectacular defeats as well. But in defeat, the Romans became more determined. They came back to reclaim victory. The story of the disaster in the Teutoburg Forest in Germany in A.D. 9 and the story of the British uprising by Boudicca of A.D. 61 show the Roman legion's ability to adapt to setbacks.

These same victories after defeat also foreshadowed the end for the Roman Empire. Rome ruled for another four hundred years, but these two defeats slowed the expansion of the empire.

REBELLION IN GERMANIA

Roman legions under Julius Caesar established the northeastern boundary of the Roman Empire in Germania at the Rhine River in 58 B.C. Germania bordered Gaul and included a good portion of what much later became Germany. In the years following the conquest, Germania had been an almost constant problem for the Romans. The Germanic tribes staged a series of revolts along the border. The Romans attempted to conquer them to create a neutral territory there. In A.D. 4, the Romans began a final push to take over the territory as far as the Elbe River to create the province of Germania. It would have equal status with Gaul, Hispania, and other provinces of the Roman Empire.

Publius Quinctillus Varus was the Roman general in charge of the Seventeenth, the Twenty-Eighth, and the Nineteenth Legions, along with cavalry and six cohorts of auxiliaries. Varus was a former proconsul (commander) of Africa. Many historians of the time felt that he was the wrong choice to lead the consolidation of the frontier. Roman historian Velleius Paterculus described him as "a man of

ROMAN CITIES ON THE WATER

Historians speak of Roman transportation in terms of roads. Roman roads were indeed a remarkable achievement. However, most ancient cities developed along waterways.

Before the Romans built roads, the only effective means of transportation was by water. By the fifth century A.D., Roman roads were no longer maintained and rapidly became unusable. Europeans returned to water as the easiest and fastest way to move people and supplies. Only in the last few hundred years have other modes of transportation overtaken waterways.

mild character and of a quiet disposition, somewhat slow in mind as he was in body, and more accustomed to the leisure of the camp than to actual service in war." As governor of this area of Germania, he was insensitive in his dealings with the local tribal leaders. He took land for new settlements, imposed taxes, and generally refused to respect their rights.

One of those leaders was Hermann (called Arminius by the Romans) of the Cherusci tribe. Arminius had lived in Rome as a child-hostage, taken to ensure peace in Germania. While in Rome, he had received training as a Roman soldier. He learned the strategies and tactics the Romans used in their battles. When he returned to

With his Roman training, Hermann knew the best ways for the Germanic tribes to fight against the Romans.

Germania at the age of twenty-five, the Romans thought they could count on him as an ally in dealing with the rebellious tribes. But in reality, he shared the anger of the tribes over the policies of Varus and took charge of their revolt. He secretly formed the tribes into an army under his command. Its mission was to permanently remove the Roman legions from the province.

While maintaining his friendship with Varus, Arminius carefully planned an ambush that would give his troops the advantage over the Roman legions. He falsely tipped off Varus to a rebellion in an area that the Romans could reach only by traveling through the Teutoburg Forest.

In A.D. 9, Arminius's troops ambushed the Roman soldiers as they marched in the rain along a narrow, muddy forest trail. They did not have enough space to form their ranks into effective fighting positions. One historian described the scene as an "increasingly chaotic and panicky mass of legionaires, cavalrymen, mules and carts." In the three-day battle that followed, the Roman legions were massacred. Varus, horrified at his losses and his loss of honor, fell upon his sword and committed suicide. Considering that he would have had to face the rage of the emperor on his return to Rome, suicide may have seemed to be his best option.

The ambush of Roman legions in the Teutoburg Forest was a shocking defeat for the Roman Empire. It came at a time when Emperor Augustus felt that the legions had established effective control of all of their conquered territories. The surprise attack by the Germanic Cherusci tribe wiped out three of Rome's legions. It was an amazing victory by a barbarian army.

Augustus sent his stepson (and future successor), Tiberius, to quell the rebellion in Germania. Six years later, after many battles, the legions under Tiberius's brother Germanicus, another Roman general,

Germanicus *(left, on a white horse)* arrives at the site of the ambush in the Teutoburg Forest in this twentieth-century French painting. He and his army found only bones and discarded weapons *(bottom left)*.

arrived at the actual site of the earlier battle. Germanicus found "the whitening bones of dead men and animals, amid fragments of their shattered weapons." Finally, the defeated soldiers could be buried.

The legions were finally successful in defeating the German tribes that had beaten Varus's soldiers. The Romans, embarrassed at the loss of three legions to barbarians, retired the numbers of those legions forever. No Roman soldier would have to serve in them again.

The Romans held what they had already conquered, but they didn't move any farther into Germania. For the first time, they had been stopped in their conquest because the price of conquest was too high. That itself was a great victory for the peoples in Germania.

THE WOMAN WHO DEFEATED THE LEGIONS

The second defeat remains one of the most intriguing stories in British history. The king of the Icenian people of Britannia, Prasutagus, died in A.D. 60 and left his territories to his daughters and the Roman emperor Nero. He hoped that the Roman conquerors of Britain would support his daughters' claim to his throne. The Romans saw his will as an excuse to take control of the late king's territories and all of its rich assets. Tacitus acknowledged that when the legions took over the area, "Kingdom and household alike were plundered like prizes of war...his widow Boudicca was flogged."

Boudicca made a bold decision to defend her daughters' rights to their father's kingdom. The Roman commander of Britannia had left the southern part of Britannia to subdue the last group of Druids, the Celtic priests who had encouraged tribal resistance to the Romans.

Boudicca speaks to the Icenian people to convince them to fight the Romans. Her three daughters sit weeping beside her.

In the commander's absence, the widowed queen of the Icenian people forged an alliance with another tribe. Together they destroyed Camulodunum (modern-day Colchester), Londinium (London), and Verulamium (Saint Albans). They also defeated the Ninth Legion, under Quintus Petillius Cerialis. This breathtaking chain of victories frightened Nero so much that he considered ordering all Roman troops from Britannia and leaving the island to its native people. Tacitus in his *Annals* called it "a serious disaster."

With the Ninth Legion defeated and the Roman procurator (local administrator), Catus Decianus, forced to flee to Gaul, the revolting tribes thought they had achieved victory. Paulinus Suetonius, governor of all Roman Britain, commanded the remaining legions.

The Icenians under Boudicca destroy the city of Londinium. They were defending the rights of their dead king's daughters to inherit the kingdom.

ROMAN COUNTING
The numbers we write—1, 2, 3, etc.—are known as Arabic numerals. Romans used a different numbering system, which we call Roman numerals. The Roman legions were designated by Roman numerals, so what we might call the Second Legion would have been II Legio.

Romans could read their numbers as easily as we read ours. Roman numerals are still seen, often in copyright notices at the end of movies and as copyright dates in older books. They are also used in countries governed by monarchs to distinguish between those with the same first name. For example, the current queen of Great Britain is Elizabeth II. Popes use the same system. The most recent pope, who picked Benedict as his name, is Benedict XVI since he is the sixteenth pope to use it.

This table shows how some of the more common numbers translate into Roman numerals:

Arabic Numeral	Roman Numeral	Arabic Numeral	Roman Numeral
1	I	8	VIII
2	II	9	IX
3	III	10	X
4	IV	50	L
5	V	100	C
6	VI	500	D
7	VII	1,000	M

He rapidly brought together an army of about ten thousand legionaries and auxiliaries to face Boudicca's forces, which according to Tacitus numbered about one hundred thousand.

Facing such a strong rebellion, Suetonius knew that he must achieve a decisive victory. He felt the natives of Britannia had to be taught that Rome could not be defied. Anything less than a total rout of the tribes and a brutal suppression of their revolt would end Roman control in Britain. Suetonius planned carefully, positioning his troops to lure Boudicca's army into a trap. He occupied a field surrounded on three sides by dense woods. This position forced Boudicca's army to attack straight into the teeth of the Roman defense.

Both leaders gave their armies emotional last-minute pep talks, and then the British charged the Roman position. Tacitus recorded the results. The British met a disciplined and better-equipped wall of Roman soldiers who "demolished all serious resistance . . . did not spare even the women. . . . [A]lmost eighty thousand Britons fell." Roman losses were around four hundred soldiers. It is not known if Tacitus's numbers are accurate, but the Roman legions had again achieved an overwhelming victory. The Battle of Watling Street, named for an ancient route (although its actual location is unknown), resulted not only in the defeat of the tribal armies but also in a large-scale massacre of Boudicca's followers.

> "[The Roman soldiers] demolished all serious resistance . . . did not spare even the women. . . . [A]lmost eighty thousand Britons fell."
>
> —Tacitus, ca. A.D. 117

BARBARIANS WHO WOULDN'T BE CIVILIZED

As in Germania, the legions had prevailed. The victory came only after a great loss of Roman life, however. The barbarians of

Britannia and Germania were not responding the way those of Gaul and Hispania had. They refused to give up their own culture, language, and religion and assume those of their conquerors. The Romans had achieved victory out of defeat this time. But ultimately the price of maintaining the empire would prove to be too much for Rome.

> "Italy has twenty-eight colonies founded under my auspices which have grown to be famous and populous during my lifetime."

—Augustus Caesar, A.D. 14

CHAPTER EIGHT

CIVILIZING AN EMPIRE

Found among Emperor Augustus's papers upon his death was an account of his accomplishments during his long reign. He proudly noted: "The number of Roman citizens who bound themselves to me by military oath was about 500,000. Of these I settled in colonies or sent back into their own towns, after their term of service, something more than 300,000, and to all I assigned lands, or gave money as a reward for military service."

This account is interesting because it indicates the number of troops serving during his reign. It shows that about 60 percent of them survived their twenty to twenty-five years of service. It is also interesting because it details what happened to the soldiers who reached retirement. One modern historian estimated, "A soldier could live comfortably on about five-sevenths of his pay." Some

These Roman copper coins date from the reign of Augustus Caesar (27 B.C. to A.D. 14).

soldiers, no doubt, spent every denarius (a Roman coin) they received for their service. Others put some aside for the future.

A GOOD RETIREMENT

With what they had saved for themselves—along with a gift of land or money from the emperor, called a donative—retired soldiers could live quite comfortably in the provinces. The cost of living was much lower there than in Rome. Four or five years before they were eligible to actually retire, legionaries were designated as veteran troops. They did not have to participate in the normal routines of camp and were called back into active service only during an emergency. During this time of less-demanding service, some soldiers might have grown food in the area surrounding their fort. Some set up themselves in trade doing the same skilled labor they had done for the past twenty or so years as soldiers. Requiring a soldier to remain where he was during his veteran years of service tended to make him stay put once he was deactivated.

THE ROMAN INTERSTATE

In 1919 Dwight Eisenhower, then a young colonel in the U.S. Army, made a trip across the United States by automobile. The purpose of his trip was to evaluate how easily people and materials could be transported across the country to defend the United States from attack. The trip took two months, a shocking amount of time. Years later, as president of the United States, Eisenhower signed legislation that authorized construction of a network of 40,000 miles (64,000 km) of interstate highways that would unite the country. The roads are called the Dwight D. Eisenhower System of Interstate and Defense Highways or the Interstate Highway System.

The Roman army knew that a good road system was critical for transporting men and materials. The Roman road network throughout the empire grew to more than 53,000 miles (85,000 km) in length and was created entirely by hand labor. Some Roman roads still exist. Some Roman bridges still carry modern pedestrian and even auto traffic.

Roman roads were built by digging a roadwide trench and filling it with rocks of various sizes to create a level surface. Laborers paved this surface with large stones that were cut to fit together precisely. The road was built slightly higher in the center so that water would drain into channels along the edges. The roads had curbs, just as modern city streets do. After Rome was conquered, these road-building techniques were lost. Historians and engineers estimate that the technology for building these roads was not duplicated in modern times until the nineteenth century.

By then, many of the soldiers had other incentives to remain in the provinces. Soldiers were not allowed to marry during their years of service. This policy did not change until very late in the history of the Roman Empire. Despite this, it was not uncommon for a soldier to quietly marry a local woman, especially as he neared retirement. After serving twenty or twenty-five years, the retiring soldier was

This stone carving from the third century A.D. shows a Roman marriage ceremony.

likely in his late thirties or early forties. With his donative, he would be a relatively wealthy man.

If he had been an auxiliary, he could also look forward to Roman citizenship, the other benefit that came with completion of military service. The right of citizenship passed on to his sons. To a local family hoping to increase its standing in its own community and with Rome, the veteran seemed like an ideal husband for a daughter.

Years away from home broke the soldier's ties to his own family. A retiring soldier would also soon lose his military family. Other friends from the legion often retired in the same area. So choosing a wife from the local community was a logical move. It gave him a new family and even more permanent ties to an area in which he may have spent most of his life.

This arrangement served the empire too. The emperor gained a built-in stabilizing force on the frontier. The soldiers who had lived the Roman life for most of their years continued to represent Rome. Their sons, as Roman citizens, would want to maintain Roman influence so as to maintain their own status. It was a perfect union of individual needs and the needs of the empire.

THE CITY OF THE EMPEROR

This retirement model was followed throughout the empire. In one case, a city was actually founded by retired veterans and named for their benefactor, Emperor Augustus. Veteran soldiers from at least the Fifth Legion and the Tenth Legion and perhaps the Twentieth Legion settled in the area. A general who had served in the legions was named as legate (administrator) for the new colony. They chose the name Emerita Augusta (modern-day Mérida, Spain) for their new town.

Augusta came from the fact that Augustus gave the land to the retiring soldiers to found the city. *Emerita* comes from the Latin word meaning "veteran." Archaeological excavations in the city revealed that native tribes had been in the area, but the Roman settlement of 25 B.C. (some say 19 B.C.) was the first permanent one. Emerita Augusta became the capital of the region of Hispania called Lusitania.

The settlement at Emerita Augusta served a military purpose for the Romans. Native tribes in that area had not been completely conquered. The settlement by the veterans brought these tribes more firmly under Roman control and culture.

Mérida remains a striking city filled with Roman ruins. It was only one of many colonies founded by legion veterans. Emperor Augustus

This Roman theater was built in the late first century B.C in Emerita Augusta, the town in Spain founded by retired legionaries and named after Augustus.

claimed credit for setting up a number of them. He described "colonies of soldiers in Africa, Sicily, Macedonia, both Spains [Spain was made up of two distinct provinces], Achaia [in Greece], Asia, Syria, Gallia [Gaul], Narbonensis [a province in southeastern Gaul], Pisidia [Antioch, Turkey]. Moreover, Italy has twenty-eight colonies founded under my auspices which have grown to be famous and populous during my lifetime."

ALWAYS WORKING FOR THE EMPIRE

The Roman soldiers were fighters. They were builders. In retirement, they became a major stabilizing and Romanizing force for the empire. They were the primary method of spreading Roman ideas and culture throughout the empire. This was their role from the time they were recruited until they died.

The Romans put enormous effort into assimilating all the peoples within their far-flung empire. On the negative side, conquered people had no choice but to accept Roman civilization and culture. What cannot be denied, however, is the efficiency and effectiveness of the system. The Roman soldier remained an instrument of the empire, a representative of Rome, long after he put away his pila and gladius.

> "[Leaders] whose shoulders may be capable of sustaining bravely the empire of the world."
>
> —Velleius Paterculus, A.D. 30

THE FALL OF THE ROMAN EMPIRE

With enlistments lagging, Emperor Septimius Severus, who reigned from A.D. 193 to 211, loosened the strict discipline of the legions. He gave the soldiers more privileges in order to attract new recruits. This more liberal treatment of the legions may have contributed to the final collapse of the empire. But the story is much more complicated than that.

LEGIONS IN DECLINE

From the time of the reforms of Marius, military service had been a great way for poor people to move up in society. As the empire continued to expand, the need for soldiers grew as well. But even the rewards offered by the military failed to produce enough recruits. By the time of Emperor Diocletian, who reigned from A.D. 284 to 305, recruitment was supplemented by conscription, or a draft. Citizens were forced into military service.

It was not a popular policy. In fact, it was so unpopular that people were willing to maim themselves or their sons to prevent them from being conscripted into the army. Even at the time of Emperor Augustus, when the legions were at their peak, one historian notes, "Augustus sold a Roman knight and his property at public auction because he had cut off the thumbs of his two young sons," thus

How Many? Why Numbers Are Slippery Things

The Romans were famous for taking censuses of their population, so it would seem that finding information about the population of the Roman Empire would be easy. But the further back in recorded history a researcher goes, the fewer sources of information there are. With fewer sources of information, the likelihood of error increases.

A great example is the Roman census. A census of the Roman world in 70 B.C. established the population at 900,000. A similar census under Emperor Augustus in 28 B.C. reported a population of 4 million. Granted, the legions had been active in acquiring new territories for the empire, but more than 3 million new inhabitants seems unlikely. The explanation is that Augustus included women and children in his census, and the earlier census had not.

Knowledgeable historians have been able to agree on only a range, rather than a specific population figure, for the world population in A.D. 1. Various estimates range from 170 million to 400 million people. With that wide a range, it is impossible to say what portion of the world population was under Roman control. Historians, in this case, have estimated the number of people living within the Roman Empire to be from 60 million to 120 million. So did Rome control 15 percent of the world's population at 60 million out of 400 million?

rendering them incapable of military service. The Roman Senate had to pass laws to deal with the problem.

Unwilling recruits proved not to be the motivated soldiers of the earlier legions. The Senate's solution was to allow more noncitizens to enlist in the regular legions. Although this policy helped increase the size of the army, it diluted the effectiveness of the legions as they became less and less subject to the strong Roman influence of the past.

This Roman relief sculpture from the late second century B.C. shows a census in progress.

Or did it control 70 percent at 120 million out of 170 million? Or should the numbers be averaged, say 30 percent of 90 million out of 285 million? The answer, of course, is that we can never know for sure.

Perhaps the simplest explanation for the fall of Rome is that the Roman Empire grew too big. Rome was unable to administer such a large and varied group of people. It was also a failure of leadership. The early Roman Empire was governed by a succession of emperors, who can be criticized for many of their decisions but not for a lack of vision. Too often the later emperors' concept of leadership meant amassing wealth and power rather than concern for the long-term welfare and continued prosperity of the Roman society as a whole.

THE VISION OF PAX ROMANA FADES

Augustus's Pax Romana was motivated by a vision of peace, in which everyone was unified into a Roman world. Although this vision oppressed native cultures, it also helped foster improvements in the daily lives of many conquered peoples. Great Roman historians such as Velleius Paterculus pleaded with the gods to continue to give the Roman people leaders "whose shoulders may be capable of sustaining bravely the empire of the world." Paterculus died before seeing the decline of the emperors that came in the years after Augustus.

It is truly amazing that the empire held together as long and as well as it did. The western part of the Roman Empire (coexistent with most of western Europe) lasted more than four hundred years, or twice as long as the United States has to date. This part of the empire survived without the instant communication and rapid transportation we take for granted. Emperors managed to govern the provinces through their personal involvement and with a relatively small group of administrators in Rome and the provinces.

Over time emperors realized that the empire had outgrown its system of government. In A.D. 286, Emperor Diocletian divided the empire into western and eastern halves to make governing more manageable. Each half had a separate government and a separate group of legions. This solution proved temporary and worked only as long as the coemperors cooperated with one another. The cooperation lasted only one generation. After that, the coemperors squabbled over power and control.

Emperor Constantine managed to pull the empire back together, uniting it as a Christian empire in A.D. 324. That connection broke down when a power struggle erupted after his death. Finally, the two halves were permanently split in A.D. 395. By that time, the eastern half of the empire, with its capital of Constantinople (modern Istanbul, Turkey), was the stronger portion. It was less threatened by outside enemies and possessed greater economic resources. The western half, with its capital in Rome, was subjected to a series of invasions by Germanic tribes. In A.D. 410, the Germanic Visigoths sacked Rome. The western portion of the empire finally came to an end sixty-six years later when the last Roman emperor was forced to resign. The eastern half of the empire lasted almost a thousand years longer.

THE EASTERN EMPIRE

It was not surprising that the eastern portion of the empire remained under Roman control for so much longer than the western portion. The eastern empire included Assyria, Mesopotamia, Palaestrina, and Arabia—much of the area that became known as the Middle East. The Parthian Empire (part of present-day Iran) dominated the region. The Parthian Empire was not strongly centralized like the Roman Empire. It was a group of kingdoms that were loosely organized for trade and defense.

The Parthian armies were cavalry armies. The Romans were an infantry-based force. Because of the Parthian cavalry, the Romans could not at first conquer this area. The two sides maintained an uneasy truce during the years of the Roman Republic. During the time of the Roman Empire, Rome again tried to subdue and annex the Parthian territories. In A.D. 116, Emperor Trajan finally took control of the area.

Over the years, disputes and conflict in the Eastern Roman Empire took place, but never the bitter fighting that occurred almost continually in the Western Roman Empire. Rome also controlled the eastern territories with a lighter hand, allowing more of the people to live as they did under the Parthians. The Eastern Roman (or Byzantine) Empire remained more peaceful and more

Emperor Trajan took control of the Parthian territories in A.D. 116.

profitable, perhaps because of the lack of conflict. It also lacked the constant threat along its borders that occurred in Britannia and Germania. In the fifth century A.D., when the western portion of the empire finally fell, it was to these German tribes. The Eastern Roman Empire—self-sufficient, prosperous, and lacking these external threats—was able to thrive for hundreds more years.

THE LEGIONS WITHDRAW

As the Roman Empire faltered, the emperors began to pull back their armies. They retreated from the farthest areas first. For those far-flung provinces, such as Britannia, the removal of the legions came at a particularly critical time. The Germanic tribes that were pressing in on Rome were also attacking Britain.

As Roman administrative control was withdrawn, some of the provinces quickly lost the veneer of Roman civilization. After the Romans had been gone from Britain for just twenty years, the people there no longer used money. They no longer imported pottery—evidence of a rapid breakdown in trade and commerce.

The roads and buildings fell in to ruin, the trade networks failed, and the Germanic tribes overran the empire. The expulsion of the last Western Roman emperor in A.D. 476 signaled the fall of the Western Roman Empire. These events ushered in the period known as the Dark Ages (A.D. 500–1500). When Europe emerged from this period, it seemed as if the Roman Empire had never existed. The civilization of the Romans, their communication and transportation networks, and their cultural and health standards had all disappeared.

At Vindolanda on Hadrian's Wall in Britain, a reconstructed portion of the Roman site includes a typical village cottage from Roman times and a villager's cottage from about one hundred years

This reconstruction of the Roman Fort Vindolanda on Hadrian's Wall in Britain shows visitors what Britain was like during and shortly after Roman occupation.

after Roman occupation ended. The differences between the basic cleanliness and quality of lifestyle are readily apparent. They illustrate the impact of the Roman withdrawal on the life of the English peasant. Rome had fallen, the legions were no more, and all they had accomplished had perished with them. Or so it must have seemed for those left behind.

> **"The Romans owed the conquest of the world to ... unwearied cultivation of the other arts of war."**
>
> —Vegetius, A.D. 390

THE ROMAN ARMY'S LEGACY

The Roman legionaries conquered an empire and held it for several hundred years. With the fall of Rome, the legions ceased to exist. But the Roman army left a legacy that will forever remain part of the societies it conquered.

THE U.S. ARMY AS A LEGION

The Roman legacy lives on in the military. The concept of citizen soldiers, which came with the development of the first legions of Rome, still exists in local militias throughout the world. At most times in U.S. history, for example, the nation did not have a professional standing army. A large army was recruited only when needed, and a small force served for defense between conflicts. When the first

The organization and policies of the U.S. military are in many ways based on the Roman model. Soldiers, such as the ones pictured above in formation, are entitled to benefits after their years of service, as were many legionaries.

permanent armies formed, they followed many of the traditions of the Roman legions of ancient history.

Because of the Roman army, modern U.S. soldiers are well paid, well trained, and well equipped. Soldiers know they are entitled to certain benefits after their terms of military service are up. They are arranged in groups (platoons, companies, brigades, divisions, and such) that vary in name from those of the Romans but create the same kind of organized chain of command. They are led by several ranks of officers that are equivalent in many respects to the Roman ranks. A Roman soldier magically transported into a modern army would obviously need training in new weaponry, but he would find the disciplined military structure very familiar.

Although the influence of the Roman legions can be seen in the modern army, it is the civilizing role of the Roman legions that had the most impact in modern lives. Roman culture still shows itself in language, architecture, and legal systems in Europe and North America. For example, because the United States was primarily settled by peoples from western Europe, the American people inherited those same Roman traditions.

THE WORDS THE ROMANS GAVE US

The impact on the languages of the empire is the most apparent. All the so-called Romance languages come from what is called vulgar (common) Latin, the language spoken by the Roman soldiers. The term *romance* when referring to language means "Romans." The languages descended from vulgar Latin are actively used in modern times are Spanish, Portuguese, French, Italian, Romanian, and Catalan (spoken in part of Spain).

Latin appears in legal terminology and even in everyday conversation in English, which has its roots in Germanic languages. Some Latin phrases are still used. For instance, the motto of the United States is E Pluribus Unum (out of many, one), which celebrates the fact that many colonies united to form one country. We hear carpe diem, or "seize the day." *Alter ego* is a common English term that means "other self" in Latin.

People who graduated from a school or college are called alumni. Some of them graduated cum laude (with honors), magna cum laude (with high honors), or summa cum laude (with highest honors). People are told to protect their own interests with the phrase *caveat emptor*, "let the buyer beware." We use fax machines to make copies, or facsimiles, of pages, from the Latin *fac simile*, "to make similar." We create monuments to our dead inscribed with *in memoriam*, "in the memory of."

We speak of income and tax numbers as *per capita*, literally "by the head," or per person. A person not allowed somewhere is labeled *persona non grata* (a person not welcome). The time from noon until midnight is P.M. or *post meridiem*, meaning "after midday."

Even English, which is not a Romance language, has a large number of words derived from Latin. *Paternal* and *maternal* come from the Latin words for "father" *(pater)* and "mother" *(mater)*. *Library* comes from *liber*, the Latin word for "book." When we address someone as "mister," we are using a derivation of the Latin word, *magister*. Our word *money* comes from *moneta*, Latin for "mint," which is the place where our coins are made.

The calendar also includes Latin words. The Romans began the new year in March, so for them September was the seventh month; October, the eighth; November, the ninth; and December, the tenth. The Latin for those numbers is *septem, octo, novem,* and *decem.* July is named for Julius Caesar and August for his successor, Emperor Augustus.

THE ARCHITECTURE OF ROME IN THE UNITED STATES

The Romans borrowed freely from those they conquered. In architecture they adopted the beautiful public spaces created by the Greeks and the obelisks (four-sided pillars) they found in Egypt. Their architecture survives, not just in the ruins found throughout their empire but also in the emphasis on ornate, monumental public buildings of marble. A quick tour of the National Mall, a park in Washington, D.C., clearly illustrates that influence.

The U.S. Capitol Building, the Washington Monument, the National World War II Memorial, and many other large marble structures illustrate the influence of Roman architecture on U.S. public buildings. And since most state capitols modeled themselves on the U.S. Capitol, the Roman influence extends to the local level.

Why Is the U.S. Capitol White?

Many public buildings in the United States *(below, the U.S. Capitol building)* and western Europe have one thing in common. They are covered with gleaming white marble like that found on the ruins of ancient Greece and Rome.

In the eighteenth century, Americans and Europeans became fascinated with these ancient civilizations, which were being rediscovered through early archaeology. Architects and designers used white marble to link the modern world with the purity and beauty of that ancient world.

The science of archaeology has advanced since those buildings were rediscovered. Chemical analysis of the Roman ruins reveals a far more colorful picture of Rome when emperors ruled their vast empire. Archaeologists and art historians have discovered that Roman buildings were once painted in vivid, bold primary colors—the same colors they used in their interior spaces. For a truer picture, modern visitors have to imagine the ancient cities in a riot of bold color.

THE INFLUENCE OF ROMAN LAW

The system of English common law and, by inheritance, the U.S. legal system also reflects Roman influence. The emperor Justinian ruled the eastern half of the Roman Empire in A.D. 534. He compiled all known Roman law into a legal code that could be used throughout the empire. That code became the basis for legal codes all over western Europe.

The code includes the writ of habeas corpus (translated as "you should have the body") used in the U.S. justice system to prevent imprisonment without evidence. It also includes defendants pleading nolo contendere, or "no contest," to charges, or police speaking of a criminal's "m.o.," or modus operandi (method of operating). The writers of the U.S. Constitution modeled the U.S. Senate on the Roman Senate—the body of elders, or *senex* in Latin. Roman influence pervades all our legal and governmental forms.

Justinian *(center)* ruled the Eastern Roman (Byzantine) Empire from A.D. 527 to 565. He organized Roman law.

From the Roman Arena to Modern Entertainment

The Roman influence may even be seen in modern pastimes and athletics. Roman soldiers played dice and card games. They also watched games in the arena and the circus (an oval racetrack). Commentators often note that football and soccer are the bloodless descendants of the gladiatorial fights in the amphitheaters of the Roman Empire. In these amphitheaters, gladiators (fighters with swords) met one another in battle, often to the death. The Colosseum in Rome was the largest and greatest of these amphitheaters. Some Roman arenas that are still standing are used for bullfighting and other sports. Not all the recreational activities were so violent, of course.

Modern horse races and auto races can trace their origin directly to the chariot races viewed by Roman emperors from their box in the Circus Maximus in Rome.

Chariot racing was a popular sport in ancient Rome. Large race tracks, such as the Circus Maximus in Rome, were built throughout the Roman world.

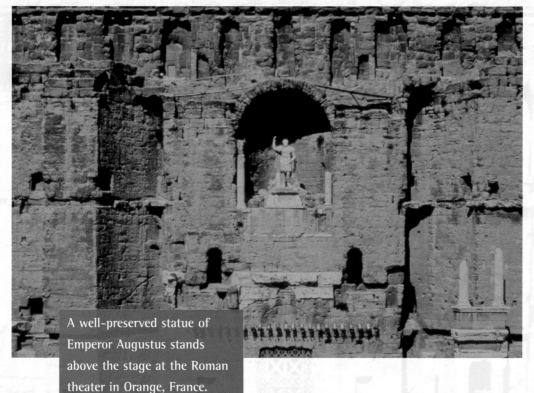

A well-preserved statue of Emperor Augustus stands above the stage at the Roman theater in Orange, France.

Remains of Roman theaters are found in many places of the former empire. Some of these are still used for concerts and plays. Attendees can sit on the uncomfortable Roman marble seats of the amphitheater in Orange, France, and see a stage performance. The statue of Emperor Augustus still watches over every scene from his niche above the stage.

The Roman legions conquered an empire for their leaders. For that they are justly remembered as great warriors. They brought professionalism to their jobs, a principle that survives in the armies of modern nations. Vegetius correctly said that "the Romans owed the conquest of the world to no other cause than continual military training, exact observance of discipline in their camps and unwearied cultivation of the other arts of war."

In their second function as civilizers and Romanizers, they exerted their greatest influence on later peoples. As historian Roger Parkinson notes, "The history of Rome is the history of the Roman legions: brutal, harsh, frightening, yet inspiring and often wise." And this history is still very much with us.

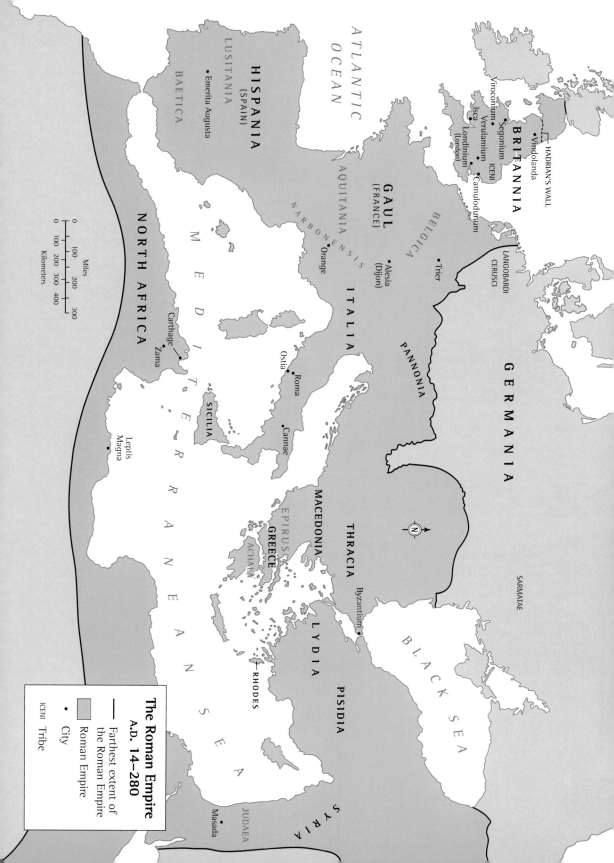

The Roman Empire
A.D. 14–280

— Farthest extent of the Roman Empire

Roman Empire

• City

ICENI Tribe

ATLANTIC OCEAN

BRITANNIA

HADRIAN'S WALL

Vindolanda

Viroconium

Segonium

Isca

Verulamium

Londinium (London)

ICENI

Camulodunum

GERMANIA

LANGOBARDI

CERUSCI

SARMATAE

Trier

BELGICA

GAUL (FRANCE)

AQUITANIA

NARBONENSIS

Orange

Alesia (Dijon)

HISPANIA (SPAIN)

LUSITANIA

BAETICA

Emerita Augusta

ITALIA

PANNONIA

Ostia

Roma

Cannae

SICILIA

NORTH AFRICA

Carthage

Zama

Leptis Magna

MEDITERRANEAN SEA

MACEDONIA

EPIRUS

GREECE

ACHAIA

THRACIA

Byzantium

LYDIA

PISIDIA

RHODES

BLACK SEA

SYRIA

JUDAEA

Masada

N

Miles
0
100
200
300

Kilometers
0
100
200
300
400

Chronology of Ancient Roman History

753 B.C.	Rome is founded.
509 B.C.	Rome becomes a republic.
146 B.C.	Rome defeats Carthage and controls the Mediterranean Sea.
107–100 B.C.	Marius reforms the citizen army.
60 B.C.	Julius Caesar, Crassus, and Pompey form the first triumvirate.
52 B.C.	At the Battle of Alesia, Julius Caesar finishes his conquest of Gaul.
49 B.C.	Julius Caesar brings his army across the Rubicon into Italy.
48 B.C.	Julius Caesar becomes absolute ruler of Rome.
44 B.C.	Julius Caesar is assassinated.
44–27 B.C.	Rome faces civil war.
27 B.C.–A.D. 14	Emperor Augustus reigns.
A.D. 9	Roman legions are routed in the Battle of the Teutoburg Forest.
A.D. 61	Boudicca revolts against the Roman legions in Britain.
A.D. 286	Emperor Diocletian divides the empire into eastern and western halves.
A.D. 324	Emperor Constantine reunites the empire.
A.D. 395	The empire is permanently divided into the Eastern Roman Empire and the Western Roman Empire.
A.D. 410	The Visigoths sack Rome.
A.D. 476	Germanic tribes depose the last Western Roman emperor.
A.D. 1453	Constantinople, capital of the Eastern Roman Empire, falls to the Ottoman Turks.

SOURCE NOTES

8 Frederick W. Shipley, trans., C. Velleius Paterculus, *Compendium of Roman History and Res Gestae Divi Augusti* (London: William Heinemann, 1924), 71.

9 John Henry Freese and other, trans., *Roman History by Titus Livius* (New York: D. Appleton and Company, 1898), xiv.

13 H. E. L. Mellersh, *The Roman Soldier* (New York: Taplinger Publishing Company, 1965), 86.

15 George Howe and Gustave Adolphus Harrer, eds., *Roman Literature in Translation* (New York: Harper & Brothers Publishers, 1924), 81.

16 Shipley, 71.

16 Bernadotte Perrin, trans., *Plutarch's Lives* (London: William Heinemann, 1920), 9:483.

20 N. P. Milner, trans., *Vegetius: Epitome of Military Science* (Liverpool: Liverpool University Press, 1993), 7.

20 Charles Freeman, *The World of the Romans* (New York: Oxford University Press, 1993), 119.

22 Milner, 7.

22 G. R. Watson, *The Roman Soldier* (London: Thames & Hudson, 1969), 55.

24 Roger Parkinson, *The Legions of Rome* (London: Wayland Publishing, 1973), 45, 47.

25 Robert F. Evans, *Legions of Imperial Rome* (New York: Vantage Press, 1980), 3.

27 Michael Grant, trans., *Tacitus: The Annals of Imperial Rome* (New York: Penguin Books, 1956), 71.

28 Time-Life Books. *What Life Was Like When Rome Ruled the World* (Alexandria, VA: Time-Life Books, 1997), 116.

31 Dyan Blacklock, *The Roman Army* (New York: Walker & Company, 2004), 12.

31 Milner, 22.

31 Ibid.

34 Time-Life Books. 116.

35 Peter Connolly, *The Roman Army* (Morristown, NJ: Silver Burdett Company, 1985), 66.

36 Gaalya Cornfeld, ed., *Josephus: The Jewish War* (Grand Rapids, MI: Zondervan Publishing House, 1982), 492.

37 Boris Rankov, *Guardians of the Roman Empire* (Oxford: Osprey Publishing, 1994), 3.

38 Robin Birley, *Roman Records from Vindolanda* (Carlisle, UK: Vindolanda Trust, 1999), 36.

38 Adrian Keith Goldsworthy, *The Roman Army at War 100 B.C.–A.D. 200* (Oxford: Clarendon Press, 1996), 283.

42 Albert Harkness, ed., *Caesar's Commentaries on the Gallic War* (New York: American Book Co., 1901), 29.

45 David J. Breeze, *Hadrian's Wall*, rev. ed. (London: English Heritage, 1993), 6-7.

46 Birley, 36.

47 Leonard A. Curchin, *Roman Spain: Conquest and Assimilation* (New York: Routledge, 1991), 97.

48 Perrin, 7:509, 511.

48 Howe and Harrer, 101.

51 Harkness, 12.

52 Howe and Harrer, 113.

52 Ibid.

52 Mellersh, 101.

55 Perrin, 7:509, 511.

55 Ibid.

60 Naphtali Lewis and Meyer Reinhold, eds., *Roman Civilization: Selected Readings*, 3rd ed. (New York: Columbia University Press, 1990), 89.

60 J. P. V. D. Balsdon, *Roman Women: Their History and Habits* (New York: Barnes & Noble Books, 1962), 18.

61 C. H. V. Sutherland, *The Romans in Spain, 217 B.C.–A.D. 117* (London: Methuen, 1939), 148.

61–62 Lewis and Reinhold, 89.

68 Grant, 328.

69–70 Shipley, 297.

71 Fergus M. Bordewich, "The Ambush That Changed History," *Smithsonian Magazine*, September 2005, available online at http://www.smithsonianmag.com/issues/2005/september/ambush.htm, 2

72 Ibid., 3.

73 Grant, 328.

74 Ibid., 327.

76 Ibid., 330–331.

76 Ibid.

78 Shipley, 393.

78 Shipley, 349.

78 H. M. D. Parker, *The Roman Legions* (Oxford: Clarendon Press, 1928), 220.

83 Shipley, 393.

85 Shipley, 329.

86 Watson, 40.

88 Shipley, 329.

93 John Clarke, trans., *Flavius Vegetius Renatus: De Re Militari* (London: W. Griffin, 1767), I.

100 Ibid.

101 Parkinson, 9.

BIBLIOGRAPHY

Adcock, F. E. *The Roman Art of War under the Republic.* Cambridge: Harvard University Press, 1940.

Baker, Patricia Ann. *Medical Care for the Roman Army on the Rhine, Danube and British Frontiers in the First, Second and Early Third Centuries A.D.* Oxford: British Archaeological Reports, 2004.

Balsdon, J. P. V. D. *Roman Women: Their History and Habits.* New York: Barnes & Noble Books, 1962.

Birley, Robin. *Roman Records from Vindolanda.* Carlisle, UK: Vindolanda Trust, 1999.

Blacklock, Dyan. *The Roman Army.* New York: Walker & Company, 2004.

Bordewich, Fergus M. "The Ambush That Changed History." *Smithsonian Magazine.* September 2005. Available online at http://www.smithsonian-mag.com/issues/2005/september/ambush.htm, 2.

Breeze, David J. *Hadrian's Wall.* Rev. ed. London: English Heritage, 1993.

Breeze, David J., and Brian Dobson. *Roman Officers and Frontiers.* Stuttgart: Franz Steiner Verlag, 1993.

Cheesman, G. L. *The Auxilia of the Roman Imperial Army.* Oxford: Clarendon Press, 1914.

Clarke, John, trans. *Flavius Vegetius Renatus: De Re Militari.* London: W. Griffin, 1767.

Connolly, Peter. *The Roman Army.* Morristown, NJ: Silver Burdett Company, 1985.

Cornfeld, Gaalya, ed. *Josephus: The Jewish War.* Grand Rapids, MI: Zondervan Publishing House, 1982.

Curchin, Leonard A. *Roman Spain: Conquest and Assimilation.* New York: Routledge, 1991.

Embleton, Ronald. *Chesters & Carrawburgh in the Days of the Romans.* Newcastle upon Tyne, UK: Frank Graham, 1985.

Erdkamp, Paul. *Hunger and the Sword: Warfare and Food Supply in Roman Republican Wars.* Amsterdam: J. G. Gieben, 1998.

Evans, Robert F. *Legions of Imperial Rome.* New York: Vantage Press, 1980.

Freeman, Charles. *The World of the Romans.* New York: Oxford University Press, 1993.

Freese, John Henry, and others, trans. *Roman History by Titus Livius.* New York: D. Appleton and Company, 1898.

Goldsworthy, Adrian Keith. *The Roman Army at War 100 B.C.–A.D. 200.* Oxford: Clarendon Press, 1996.

Grant, Michael. *Army of the Caesars.* New York: Barnes & Noble Books, 1974.

——. trans. *Tacitus: The Annals of Imperial Rome*. New York: Penguin Books, 1956.

Griffiths, W. B. *Segedunum: Roman Fort, Baths & Museum*. Newcastle upon Tyne, UK: Tyne and Wear Museums, 2000.

Harkness, Albert, ed. *Caesar's Commentaries on the Gallic War*. New York: American Book Co., 1901.

——. *The Military System of the Romans*. New York: D. Appleton and Company, 1887.

Howe, George, and Gustave Adolphus Harrer, eds. *Roman Literature in Translation*. New York: Harper & Brothers Publishers, 1924.

Lewis, Naphtali, and Meyer Reinhold, eds. *Roman Civilization: Selected Readings*. 3rd ed. New York: Columbia University Press, 1990.

Liberati, Anna Maria, and Fabio Bourbon. *Ancient Rome: History of a Civilization That Ruled the World*. Vercelli, It.: White Star, 1996.

Martínez, José Alvarez, and others. *Mérida*. León, Spain: Editorial Everest, S.A., n.d.

Matyszak, Philip. *The Enemies of Rome*. London: Thames & Hudson, 2004.

Mellersh, H. E. L. *The Roman Soldier*. New York: Taplinger Publishing Company, 1965.

Milner, N. P., trans. *Vegetius: Epitome of Military Science*. Liverpool: Liverpool University Press, 1993.

Nicasie, M. J. *Twilight of Empire*. Amsterdam: J. C. Gieben, 1998.

Parker, H. M. D. *The Roman Legions*. Oxford: Clarendon Press, 1928.

Parkinson, Roger. *The Legions of Rome*. London: Wayland Publishing, 1973.

Peddie, John. *The Roman War Machine*. Conshohocken, PA: Combined Books, 1994.

Perrin, Bernadotte, trans. *Plutarch's Lives*. Vol. 9. London: William Heinemann, 1920.

Rankov, Boris. *Guardians of the Roman Empire*. Oxford: Osprey Publishing, 1994.

Salway, Peter. *The Oxford Illustrated History of Roman Britain*. Oxford: Oxford University Press, 1993.

Shipley, Frederick W., trans. *C. Velleius Paterculus, Compendium of Roman History and Res Gestae Divi Augusti*. London: William Heinemann, 1924.

Shochat, Yanir. *Recruitment and the Programme of Tiberius Gracchus*. Brussels: Latomus, 1980.

Simkins, Michael. *Legions of the North*. Oxford: Osprey Publishing, 1979.

——. *The Roman Army from Caesar to Trajan*. Reading, England: Osprey Publishing Ltd., 1974.

——. *Warriors of Rome*. London: Blandford Press, 1988.

Southern, Pat, and Karen Ramsey Dixon. *The Late Roman Army*. New Haven, CT: Yale University Press, 1996.

Sutherland, C. H. V. *The Romans in Spain, 217 B.C.–A.D.117*. London: Methuen, 1939.

Time-Life Books. *What Life Was Like When Rome Ruled the World*. Alexandria, VA: Time-Life Books, 1997.

Watson, G. R. *The Roman Soldier*. London: Thames & Hudson, 1969.

Webster, Graham. *The Roman Army*. Chester, UK: Grosvenor Museum, 1956.

Wells, Peter S. "The Battle That Stopped Rome: Emperor Augustus, Arminius, and the Slaughter of the Legions in the Teutoburger Forest." *Mankind Quarterly* 44, no. 2 (March 2003): 246–250

For Further Information

Books

Blacklock, Dyan. *The Roman Army: The Legendary Soldiers Who Created an Empire*. New York: Walker Books for Young Readers, 2004.

Butterfield, Moira, and Mark Bergin. *Going to War in Roman Times*. New York: Franklin Watts, 2000.

Day, Nancy. *Your Travel Guide to Ancient Greece*. Minneapolis: Twenty-First Century Book, 2001.

DuTemple, Lesley A. *The Colosseum*. Minneapolis: Twenty-First Century Book, 2003.

Markle, Rita J. *The Fall of the Roman Empire*. Minneapolis: Twenty-First Century Books, 2008.

——. *Your Travel Guide to Ancient Rome*. Minneapolis: Lerner Publications Company, 2004.

Mellor, Ronald, and Marni McGee. *The Ancient Roman World*. New York: Oxford University Press, 2004.

Nardo, Don. *Life of a Roman Soldier*. San Diego: Lucent Books, 2000.

——. *The Roman Army: Instrument of Power*. San Diego: Lucent Books, 2003.

Sherman, Josepha. *Your Travel Guide to Ancient Israel*. Minneapolis: Twenty-First Century Book, 2004.

Shuter, Jane. *Life in a Roman Fort*. Oxford: Heinemann, 2005.

Woods, Michael, and Mary B. Woods. *Ancient Transportation*. Minneapolis: Twenty-First Century Books, 2000.

——. *Ancient Warfare*. Minneapolis: Twenty-First Century Books, 2000.

Websites

Fordham University
http://www.fordham.edu
Fordham University has put all the major Roman historical works online in one place. Search for information about Augustus, Caesar, Livy, Plutarch, and Tacitus.

Hadrian's Wall Country
http://www.hadrians-wall.org/
This tourism website includes introductions to Hadrian's Wall and the Roman ruins, with many photos of the area.

Illustrated History of the Roman Empire: The Roman Army
http://www.roman-empire.net/army/army.html
This great general site contains lots of detailed information on the Roman Empire and on the organization of the Roman army.

INDEX

About the Author

Susan Provost Beller is the author of twenty history books for young readers. She writes from her home in Charlotte, Vermont, when she is not either traveling to see historic sites or visiting with her three children and five grandchildren. Her one wish is that someone would invent a time machine so she could go back and really see the past!

Photo Acknowledgments